With a deep whump, the air around them was sucked toward the ravine.

A wall of heat soared. Flames engulfed the car.

The heat blast brought Buck to his senses. He released Jeff. "Start the pump!"

Buck ran to the back of the truck and yanked a hose down. He moved partway down the ravine, showering a broad spray of water on the burning car. Feeding on the gasoline, the flames laughed at his feeble efforts.

Soon Jeff stood beside him, another hose in hand. Together they battered back the fire until it diminished into a wide band of gray smoke. Both men had to turn away from what they saw.

ROSEY DOW
AND
ANDREW SNADEN
first teamed up to write *Betrayed,* a novel of suspense. A 2001 Christy Award winner, Rosey lives in Mississippi where she and her husband are church planters. The family worked for many years in Grenada as missionaries. Andrew lives on a farm in British Columbia and works as an accountant.

Books by Rosey Dow

HEARTSONG PRESENTS
HP204—Megan's Choice
HP299—Em's Only Chance
HP491—An Unexpected Surprise

Flames
of Deceit

Rosey Dow
and Andrew Snaden

Heartsong Presents

To our daughters.

A note from the author:
We love to hear from our readers! You may correspond with us by writing:

Rosey Dow and Andrew Snaden
Author Relations
PO Box 719
Uhrichsville, OH 44683
www.roseydow.com

ISBN 1-58660-611-5

FLAMES OF DECEIT

Cover illustration by Ron Hall.

PRINTED IN THE U.S.A.

one

Buck Connelly flipped on the fire truck's emergency equipment, then jammed down the accelerator. The diesel motor revved up, but like an overladen mule, the fire truck lumbered out of the Muskrat Creek Volunteer Fire Department, its roar greater than its speed. It turned the corner onto the highway, passing a poplar tree that still held on to a few yellow leaves. Soon winter would bark on the heels of autumn.

The pumper truck picked up speed. Buck glanced over at his husky partner and friend of twenty years, Jeff Thompson. Grim-faced, Jeff strapped on his helmet. The light blue of his conservation officer's uniform poked out underneath his turnout gear. Buck ranched for a living, and Jeff controlled the wild game of the Cariboo region of British Columbia.

"I can't believe only two of us showed up," Jeff yelled over the blaring siren.

"The joy of belonging to a volunteer department," Buck called back. "Hopefully some more guys will show up later. 911 has already dispatched the rescue truck from Area D."

"Good, we'll probably need it. If this is anything like the last highway wreck, we'll need the Jaws of Life to pry open the car."

Buck nodded. "Let's hope not." The last accident claimed the lives of an elderly woman and her ten-year-old grandson. Located on the Old Cariboo Highway in the central region of British Columbia, Muskrat Creek Volunteer Fire Department saw a lot of car accidents.

The fire truck soon approached a crowd milling about on

the side of the road. Buck slowed, navigating past the vehicles parked haphazardly along the side of the road.

"I hope they left a place for us," Jeff said.

"No kidding. I think we spend just as much time controlling traffic as we do fighting fires in this job. You'd think people could figure it out for themselves." Buck brought the truck to a halt on the edge of the highway and killed the motor and siren. From the side window, he could see a dark blue car resting at the bottom of a steep embankment.

Jeff leaned over him to look out too. "That's gotta be at least thirty feet down."

Buck sighed and reached for his door handle. "Great. There's nothing like a rescue on the side of a hill."

"Makes you feel warm and fuzzy, doesn't it?"

Their doors came open, and the two firefighters jumped down. The dozen onlookers hovered around the truck. "People!" Buck said. "We need you to move back at least fifty feet. Those of you with cars parked have to move them as well."

The crowd grumbled and stepped back ten feet.

"Rocket scientists," Jeff said.

Buck pointed to a bulky trucker standing in the crowd. "You. We don't have time for this. Get these people and their vehicles out of our hair."

The big man grinned. Swiveling, he spread heavy arms and rumbled, "Okay, everybody back. Give these gentlemen room to work." The crowd grumbled some more but obeyed. Cars started and moved. People stepped away.

Buck went to the edge of the embankment and looked down. The dry, yellow autumn grass covered the earth all the way to the bottom. Crunched on all sides, the vehicle rested right side up at the bottom of the ravine. Buck's gut tightened when he saw a black high-voltage power line across the hood.

Buck tensed. The power line was like a snake, lying in wait for prey to come close enough. When it did, the snake would strike out, tearing into the poor soul who ventured near. Buck started to sweat, and his knees weakened. He pulled his attention away from the power line and clenched his hands to stop them from trembling.

Looking closer at the Crown Victoria in the ravine, Buck saw a man's head slumped against the steering wheel. The hair was blond, but most of it was dark and matted with fresh blood. The side of the face that could be seen was battered and bloody.

Jeff squinted. "Is that who I think it is?"

"Yeah. Garret Simmons."

The power line taunted him, and the sight of Garret Simmons ripped open an old wound that never healed. Buck only loved one woman in his life, and through his own stupidity, he pushed her away. A year later, Alicia married Garret Simmons. Buck felt no anger toward Garret. From all reports, he treated Alicia well. Buck just felt that constant aching of love lost, one that would never be found again.

Jeff tapped his elbow and pointed to a pool of liquid forming under the smashed vehicle. "The fuel tank must've been ruptured. We better get down there pronto."

"Right." Buck stepped forward, and his vision blurred. Did that line move? He willed his legs to go, but his feet were rooted firmly to the ground.

Jeff stopped, turned, and faced him. "Come on."

The power line mesmerized Buck. He could see it slashing out, jamming its volts of electricity into whoever was foolish enough to step into its grasp. "I can't."

Jeff searched his face and stepped up to him. "Hey, you're not freezing on me, are you?"

Buck glanced around, thankful the fire truck shielded them

from the prying eyes of the onlookers. "I just can't race down there."

Jeff grimaced. "I thought you said you were over 100 Mile House?"

"I thought so too."

Jeff looked back at the ravine, then turned his face toward Buck. "Okay, you stay here. I'll get him myself."

Jeff turned to go down the embankment, but Buck grabbed his arm.

"What are you doing?" Jeff demanded.

Buck held Jeff's arm in a no-nonsense grip. That power line didn't care which one of them it got, as long as its hunger was satisfied. He must protect Jeff. "It's not safe."

"Safe? Since when has fire fighting been safe? Come on, Buck. Let me pull him out of there. The car's still running. Any second now, that gas could ignite."

Buck tightened his grip. "And if that power line is alive, you'll fry."

Jeff looked over his shoulder, surveying the line and the fallen power pole. "Nah, it's dead. The transformer's all smashed, and the switch popped. I'll be okay. Just stay here, and I'll take care of it."

Jeff moved to pull away, but Buck applied more force and held him firm. "Stay here. We'll call for the power company and make sure the line is dead before we approach the scene. That's proper procedure anyways."

Jeff spun hard to jerk free from Buck's grip. "Let me go! Garret Simmons hasn't got time for proper procedure."

Buck pulled Jeff tight against him, wrapping his arm around his friend's neck. Sweat popped from Buck's forehead, but like a professional wrestler, he would not let Jeff squirm free. He would not let the snake below do to Jeff what it had done to him.

Jeff grunted. "I'll be okay, Buck. Let me help him."

Buck held tight, but then the argument was settled for them.

With a deep *whump,* the air around them was sucked toward the ravine. A wall of heat soared. Flames engulfed the car.

The heat blast brought Buck to his senses. He released Jeff. "Start the pump!"

Jeff disappeared around to the other side of the truck to work the pump controls. Buck ran to the back of the truck and yanked a hose down. He dragged it to the ravine's edge. The pump cut in, and the hose charged with water. Buck moved partway down the ravine, showering a broad spray of water on the burning car. Feeding on the gasoline, the flames laughed at his feeble efforts.

Soon Jeff stood beside him, another hose in hand. Together they battered back the fire until it diminished into a wide band of gray smoke. Both men had to turn away from what they saw.

"Who's going to tell his wife?" Jeff asked, after a few moments of grim silence.

"I guess I will," Buck answered. He felt light-headed. He had to sit down for a minute.

≈

In the living room of her spacious colonial home, Alicia Simmons scooped a pile of crumpled pink tissues off the teak coffee table, went into the kitchen, and dropped them into the garbage can. Two hours had passed since Garret left, and Alicia had pretty much cried herself out. As usual, the fight started over something trivial. He wanted his light blue dress shirt for the council meeting that night, and she forgot to iron it.

He'd held up the wrinkled shirt like it was the convicting evidence in a court case. "What do you do all day, anyway?"

She shot back, "I've been looking after *your* daughter,

cleaning *your* house, washing *your* clothes, and cooking *your* meals!" That was all it took to start the bullets flying.

Alicia blew her nose and dropped another tissue into the trash can. She knew the shirt wasn't the real issue. Garret's growing political career kept him away from home. Alicia felt like a widow who still cooked meals for her deceased husband—when he bothered to come home to eat them. Any chance to be in the public's eye took priority with Garret.

Behind her a sweet voice asked, "You okay now, Mommy?"

Alicia looked down into the big blue eyes of her eight-year-old daughter. "Yes, Sally. I'm okay."

Her daughter's pained face tore at Alicia's heart. At the first sign of the fight, Sally bolted to her room. She used to cry when they started fighting. Now she hid. How much damage had they already done to their daughter? Alicia took Sally's hand and led her to the living room sofa. She sat down and eased her daughter onto her lap. Sally rested her pixie face against Alicia's neck. "Are you and Daddy getting divorced?"

Alicia stroked her daughter's long, dark hair. "Of course not, Honey. Why would you think that?"

"Billy Baker's parents yell at each other all the time, and he said they're getting divorced."

Alicia gently pushed her daughter back and held her little face in both hands. Sally's eyes brimmed with tears. Her lower lip quivered.

"I know Daddy and I yell at each other sometimes, but that doesn't mean we're getting divorced. We love each other very much."

"Billy said his parents used to love each other, but the love went away."

Alicia stroked her daughter's satin cheek. "That was Billy's parents, not Daddy and me."

Sally bit her lower lip.

"What is it, Honey?"

"Do you think you might stop loving me some day?"

Alicia grabbed Sally close. Her heart thundered, condemning her. How could she and Garret allow their selfishness to hurt this sweet child? "Don't ever think that, Sally. We will always love you."

"Even if you and I start yelling at each other?"

Alicia turned Sally's head upward and locked eyes with her daughter. She leaned forward until their noses almost touched. "Nothing will ever make me stop loving you. Nothing. Do you believe me?"

Sally nodded.

Alicia hugged her daughter and only let go when a knock sounded at the door. "Get yourself a cookie from the cabinet, Honey. I'll be in to get you some milk in a moment."

Her tears forgotten, Sally skipped to the kitchen. Alicia got to her feet. Before opening the heavy maple door, she paused by the mirror in the hall. She brushed aside a strand of honey-blond hair that stuck to her flushed cheek. Grabbing a handful of pink tissues from the box by the door, she dabbed her eyes and blotted her face. Her fingers wrapped around the door handle and pulled. The door was halfway open when she froze.

There stood Buck Connelly in his fire fighting gear. That familiar surge of attractive energy hit her when she saw him. She'd almost forgotten how much his rugged face, dimpled chin, and deep blue eyes affected her. She hadn't seen Buck for almost a year and then just a glimpse across a parking lot. She pushed the thoughts back. The fight had made her vulnerable.

He smiled awkwardly. "Hi, Alicia. Can I come in?"

She stiffened. What would Garret think if he heard Buck had come around? And why was Buck standing there anyway? Since their breakup ten years ago, their relationship had been nothing more than awkward greetings whenever their paths happened to cross.

"Uh, I don't think that would be proper, Buck," she stammered. She drew in a breath and tried to steady her words. "What do you want, anyway?" There was an edge to her voice. She'd never been comfortable with how things ended between them.

"I really think we should talk inside," he said as he slipped stocking feet out of his bulky rubber boots.

Alicia placed her hand against the doorjamb to block his way. "I'm sure anything you've got to say can be said at the door."

He looked down, his jaw taut.

"What is it, Buck?" She was starting to get scared.

He let out a quick breath. "Alicia. . .Garret."

Cold fear crept down her back. It suddenly struck her that Buck was standing at her door in firefighter's gear. She started to tremble. "What's happened?" It was a shrill squeak.

Buck blurted out. "Garret died in a car accident about half an hour ago."

Suddenly, Buck became a blur. Everything spun. Her knees buckled, and blackness closed in.

❧

Buck jumped forward and caught Alicia as her eyes rolled backwards. He easily scooped her slender frame into his arms and carried her into the house. She was as beautiful as always. Alicia had blond hair, creamy skin, and hazel eyes. Her full lips naturally curved up at the corners, even when she was angry. Right now, her face was pale, and he needed to set her down.

As Buck rounded the corner into Alicia's living room, her foot caught a brass picture frame, and it crashed to the floor. He'd clean that up later.

The room ahead of him smelled of money. The cream-colored carpet felt knee-deep. The left wall had a recessed alcove containing a small, dark statue of a gazelle in full stride. It was a contemporary room containing teak tables and polished pewter lamps with black shades. A long, white sofa sat before a fireplace with two deep, navy lounge chairs on either side of the hearth.

Suddenly, a little girl wearing jeans and a red sweatshirt charged into the room. At the sight of her unconscious mother hanging limply in Buck's arms, the child skidded to a stop. "What did you do to my mommy?"

Buck froze. "It's okay," he said, trying to sound soothing. "She fainted. I just caught her before she fell down and hurt herself."

The child's tiny fists came up. "Put her down, or I'll bop you." She circled him, fire in her eyes.

"I'll just lay her on the sofa." He gently placed Alicia on the couch, eased her head down on the soft, rounded sofa arm, then squatted to talk to the girl.

She still had a gleam in her eyes. Accusingly she said, "You're a stranger."

Buck smiled and spoke softly. "I'm a firefighter. I help people. My name's Buck Connelly." He held out his hand to shake.

"You're a stranger." The child bolted past him, flew to her mother, and buried her face in Alicia's neck. "Mommy! Wake up!"

Alicia's hand came up to touch the child's back. "Sally?" she mumbled. "Sally? Let me breathe, Honey."

Buck stood. This was awkward.

Alicia sat up. She seemed dazed. Her eyes went to Buck, and she gasped, "Oh, no, it's true." She held one hand over her eyes and sobbed.

Sally's mouth dropped open. She grabbed her mother's arm. "What happened, Mommy? Why is this stranger here?"

Alicia pulled her arm loose from her daughter's grip and encircled her shoulders. Between sobs, she gasped, "Something terrible happened."

Sally touched her mother's wet face. "What, Mommy?"

"A car accident," Alicia managed to say. "He died, Sally. He's gone."

Sally's face turned red. "It's not true," she shouted. "You're lying. Daddy's left us. You always yelled at him so he ran away!" Sally pushed herself away from Alicia until she broke free. She ran down the short hallway and up the stairs.

Alicia struggled to her feet and swayed. Buck placed a hand beneath her elbow, steadying her. "I have to go to her," Alicia said.

Like a ghost, Alicia floated down the hall. Buck followed, not sure what to do, but knowing Alicia needed him. They went up the stairs to Sally's room. Buck stopped at the door; Alicia went in. The child lay sprawled on a white princess bed, her face buried deep in a pillow that muffled her sobs. Alicia sat on the edge of Sally's bed, rubbing her daughter's back.

Sally turned her face upward. "Go away! I hate you!"

Alicia rocked, as if a bullet had struck her.

"Go away!"

She stood, stepped back, and turned toward Buck, her eyes pleading for help.

"Let me talk to her," Buck said.

Alicia retreated to the doorway.

Buck lowered himself onto the edge of the bed. What could he ever say to ease this kind of pain? "Sally, I need to talk to you."

"Leave me alone," Sally said into the pillow.

"Please?"

"I want my Daddy!" Sobs wracked Sally's body. Alicia moaned from the door.

Buck could only do what his mother did when he'd been a child and afraid. Buck softly stroked Sally's hair and sang, "Jesus Loves Me" until she cried herself to sleep. He pulled a comforter nestled on the end of the bed over her. He studied Sally's angelic face. Other than her dark hair, she was the image of her mother.

Buck eased himself off the bed and turned toward the door. Alicia was a pale shell. He followed her back down the stairs to the living room. She sat on the sofa and stared at the wall, her hands knotted together in her lap. He sat in the easy chair across from her. Silence passed between them for five full minutes.

"Thanks for taking care of Sally," she said, her voice flat.

"She's a beautiful child."

More silence.

"Garret and I had a fight," Alicia said, as though taking up a story she'd just left off.

"I figured as much."

Tears dripped from her chin as she continued, "He was so angry. He drove out of here like a maniac." She turned toward Buck. "That's what killed him, wasn't it?"

Buck hesitated. "The police are still investigating."

"But you have an idea, don't you?" She dashed at her eyes and squinted at him, waiting for him to answer.

He swallowed and tried to get a grip, trying not to let Alicia's tortured face rip his heart apart. She hurt, and he couldn't let her suffer. "Alicia, it's a tricky section of the highway. It could've been a deer, a moose—maybe he was cut off. You shouldn't blame yourself. It was probably just an accident."

Alicia shook her head and rubbed pink tissues across her

face. They joined a growing mound on the coffee table. "I killed him. If I'd told him I was sorry for not having his stupid blue shirt ironed, everything would be all right. But I didn't. I had to get the fight going. Because of that, Garret. . ." She let out an animal-like cry and bent over until her face almost touched her knees.

Buck got up from his seat and knelt before her. "Alicia, don't torment yourself. A deer could have run in front of the car. This won't help you. . .or Sally."

She looked up at him as though grasping for a thin lifeline. At that second, he knew he had to tell her what really happened. It wasn't her fault Garret was dead. It was his. He opened his mouth, but he couldn't force out the words. Alicia couldn't be more than a breath away from a complete nervous breakdown. Knowing there might have been a chance to save Garret could push her over the edge. He'd tell her, soon, when she could take it. But Buck wondered if he could take it. . . . He drew in a shaky breath and stood. "I need to get back to the scene. There's still some cleanup to do."

Alicia grabbed his hand. "How did he die, Buck? I've got to know! Did he suffer?"

Buck tensed, looking at the floor.

"What happened, Buck?"

"He was unconscious. . .when the car exploded. He didn't know what hit him."

Alicia started to shake. Buck reached out and drew her close, while her slight frame wracked with sobs. Hot shame washed over him, and he eased her back.

"I don't want to leave you alone," he said, when her crying eased some.

"I'll be okay," she said. "I think being alone is the best thing right now."

He reached for his wallet. "Here's my card." He handed

her a white rectangle with red letters on it. "Call me if you need anything at all. Day or night."

Nodding, she laid it on the coffee table and stared at the wooden surface. She didn't get up to see him out.

Starting the red pickup he'd borrowed from a friend at the accident scene, Buck backed out of Alicia's driveway. His love for Alicia burned brightly. He'd visited lots of families, gave lots of bad news, had lots of tears cried in front of him. No tears wrenched his heart like Alicia's. With that awareness came black despair. What would she think of him when she learned the truth about Garret's death?

two

About two miles from his destination, Buck came to the end of a line of traffic. Until the police finished their investigation, the highway would remain closed. Pulling to the shoulder, Buck eased past the waiting vehicles. The firefighter controlling the traffic gave him a nod as he passed the head of the line and parked across from his own fire truck.

Buck was a weary man when he emerged from the Blazer. Though the corpse had been removed, the burned-out wreck seemed to yell, *Coward!* at him. Buck Connelly had caused Alicia's and Sally's tears.

Jeff came around from the side of the fire truck. He drew up when he saw Buck. "How did it go?"

"Good." Buck said abruptly.

Jeff stared at him. "She's okay with what happened?"

Staring at the wreckage below, Buck didn't answer.

"She's not upset?" Jeff prodded.

"Of course she's upset," Buck snapped. "She's handling it as well as can be expected."

Jeff put up his hands as though holding Buck off. "Hey, take it easy. I just figured she'd blow up when she found out what happened."

Eyes narrowed, Buck edged closer to Jeff. "What are you getting at?"

Jeff stepped back. "Well. . .you know, stopping me from trying to start a rescue."

Buck's shoulders suddenly sagged. "I didn't tell her."

"You didn't tell her?" Jeff shook his head. "If she ever. . ."

18

"What are you guys talking about?" a gruff voice interrupted.

Both of them turned to face Rick Dupre, the tall, lean captain of the rescue team. He had a short, salt-and-pepper beard and a heavy scowl. "Were you guys thinking about going down there with that power line on the car?"

"Uh, we'd considered it," Jeff hedged.

Dupre boomed, "Don't ever approach a vehicle with a power line down until the power company tells you it's dead."

"It looked dead," protested Jeff. "The transformer was smashed and. . ."

"Doesn't matter," Dupre interrupted. He looked at Jeff as though not believing his ears. "The power isn't off until BC Hydro says it's off. We don't kill firefighters to rescue accident victims. Ever."

Jeff Thompson's mouth quirked. "That's stupid. Sometimes we can see for ourselves that it's dead."

Dupre stepped in until he was chin to chin with Jeff. "Stupid or not, it's policy. If you don't like the policy, resign. We're all volunteers. We do it by the book."

Thompson ground out, "Tell that to Alicia Simmons." He stormed off down the hill toward the wrecked car.

Dupre shook his head and turned to Buck. "He's a bit of a hothead, isn't he?"

Buck shook his head. "No, he's a good guy. Honestly, he's probably right. It was pretty obvious the line was dead. We should've gone down."

"Connelly, don't even think about it," Dupre said, getting heated. "I know you've been doing this for years, but what I said to him goes for you too. We don't approach when there's a power line. Accept it or quit. After what happened at 100 Mile House, I figured you, of all people, would know better. We clear?" He marched away without waiting for a reply.

At the mention of 100 Mile House, Buck got the shakes.

That accident happened three-and-a-half hours south of their community. On his way home from a cattle sale, Buck was the first on the accident scene. Clearly, he had no time to wait for the local rescue truck. Buck went down by himself. When he came back up, he wasn't the same man. He lost the edge that night, and Garret Simmons died because of it.

"What a mess."

A sad, husky voice beside him brought him out of his thoughts. Buck looked up at Ronny Howell, a member of the Royal Canadian Mounted Police. The good-natured red-head had worked with Buck on many an accident, and they'd become friends. Young and powerfully built, Howell towered over Buck.

"Any idea of cause?" Buck asked.

The RCMP constable rubbed the back of his wide neck. "It looks like he missed the curve and drove off the highway. There are no skid marks to indicate he tried to stop. Based on the distance the car must've traveled in the air, he took that curve at sixty miles an hour. It's only rated for thirty."

"That's crazy," Buck said. "Everyone knows this is a dangerous curve. There are three warning signs for it."

Howell shrugged. "Maybe he didn't want to slow down, or maybe he couldn't."

"I don't get it."

Howell's expression tightened. "Buck, we're treating this as suspicious. Late at night, we'd assume he'd fallen asleep; but during a sunny afternoon, we have to consider other possibilities such as brake failure. The guys back at Prince George will have the vehicle checked out for that one. Or. . ."

"What?"

"Suicide. A car wreck is a good way to go. It looks like an accident, and your wife has no hassles with the life insurance company."

Buck shook his head. "Nah. No way. Simmons had it made. He held a seat on the council and was blessed with a great little family. . . ."

Howell knit his eyebrows together. "I heard you informed the wife. How did she take it?"

"She fainted."

"That's encouraging. A woman doesn't faint if she hates her husband. She didn't happen to say anything about Simmons's state of mind did she?"

Buck paused. What if he told Howell that Alicia and Garret had been fighting? How would he interpret it? Would it ruin Alicia's chances of collecting life insurance if the death was ruled a suicide? But he had to be honest. "They'd been fighting. She said he was furious when he left."

"In that case, he was probably preoccupied with his domestic troubles and missed the curve."

"It doesn't mean suicide?"

"Nah," Howell said. "With suicide, the guy leaves quietly or in tears, not angry. If the inspection of the vehicle doesn't show anything else, we'll write it up as accidental. The coroner may or may not want to hold a hearing."

Buck froze at the thought of a coroner's hearing. If that happened, everyone involved would have to testify to the events surrounding the accident. That meant everyone, including Alicia, would know he'd stopped Jeff from trying to save Garret Simmons.

Buck cleared his throat. "How likely is that?"

"Based on what I've seen and heard, not much. Well, I gotta get back and start writing reports. See ya later."

"Yeah," Buck said.

Since all the hoses and other gear had been picked up by volunteers who arrived on the scene later, Buck wearily hauled himself into the cab of his fire truck and waited for Jeff to return. What a day. Did they come any worse than this?

The passenger door opened, and Jeff climbed in. Despite the chilly November weather, he was sweaty from the crawl up the hill in full gear. "Sorry," Jeff said.

"Huh?" Buck came out of his thoughts and stared at his partner.

"While I was down at the wreck, some of the guys were telling me stories about power lines energizing by something called induction. They take power from the lines running above them so that even though they look dead, they aren't. You did the right thing. I should've known you wouldn't have stopped me without a good reason."

"Not a problem." Buck reached for the starter. "Let's get back to the hall and see what Karen's got cooking."

Buck gave a blast of the air horn and pulled out onto the highway.

As they moved down the road, Buck called, "What did the guys think about our little scuffle on the hill?"

"They don't know about it," Jeff said. "I figured that should stay between you and me."

Buck glanced over at Jeff. "Thanks."

"No, Partner," Jeff replied. "Thank *you*."

❧

Buck pulled the fire truck into the hall, shut off the motor, and sighed. They'd both been pretty quiet on the ride back. "What a day."

"Yeah," Jeff said. "I hope we never see another one like that."

"Me either."

They hauled themselves out of the truck, went over to the closets lining the wall, and stripped off their gear. Buck followed Jeff to the door that led to the recreation hall next door. Karen, the department's secretary, would have snacks for them. The guys always needed time to unwind after a fatality. Karen was another problem in Buck's catastrophic love life. At one point, he thought he was over Alicia and had dated Karen. They'd grown serious—serious enough for him to propose and for her to accept. He called the wedding off.

Not too long before their wedding date, he'd seen Alicia at a hockey game. She was in the stands on the other side of the rink. His gaze kept flitting from the game to her. That was when Buck knew she was still firmly entrenched in his heart. He couldn't make a marriage vow to Karen, when he still loved Alicia.

Karen had taken it well. At least, he thought she did. There were no tears when he announced his decision, though Buck was sure there'd been some later. He'd cried, so Karen must have, but they were friendly with each other, and Karen had even found love again. She was dating Jeff. Still, sometimes when Karen looked at him, Buck saw something in her eyes—not hurt, but something else.

They entered the recreation hall. To the left was a pool table, the site of many good-natured contests. Directly across from Buck were two long tables end to end, able to seat sixteen men. Off to the right was a kitchen. Karen emerged from the kitchen with a pot of coffee in her hand. "Hey, you're the first back."

"We let the other guys clean up," Jeff said.

Karen knit her dark eyebrows together. She surveyed Jeff's face, then her gaze fell on Buck before returning to Jeff. "What happened?"

"It was a fatality," Jeff said. He walked over to the table and slumped into a chair.

She stared after him, then turned toward Buck. "Who was in the car?"

"Garret Simmons," Buck said softly.

Karen lost her breath for a second. "Garret Simmons?"

Buck slumped into a chair. "Yeah." He rubbed his face and said between his fingers, "His car burst into flames."

Karen put her hand to her mouth. "That's horrible. Poor Alicia."

When Karen mentioned Alicia's name, it was almost like an afterthought. He couldn't blame her. Karen probably saw Alicia as the woman who had stood between her and happiness. Buck felt terribly uncomfortable. All he wanted to do was leave. He got up from the chair. "I think I'll head home."

Jeff glanced up at him. "Sure."

"Talk to you later. See ya, Karen."

"Sure," she said, her focus more on Jeff.

Buck trudged to the door and pushed it open.

"Today was one close call," he heard Jeff say to Karen, as the door swung shut behind him.

❧

Staff Sergeant Larry Meyers of the Prince George RCMP hunched his six-foot-two-inch frame under the hoist that held up the burned-out wreck of Garret Simmons's car. Using his flashlight, he inspected the blackened and twisted metal underneath. "So he just drove straight off the curve?"

"That's right, Sir," Ronny Howell answered. "There were no skid marks, and the vehicle went quite a distance before hitting the side of the embankment."

"What's the victim's name?" Meyers probed the blackened shell before him.

"Garret Simmons."

Meyers paused to look at Howell. "The guy on the regional district council?"

"Same."

Turning back to his work, Meyers fiddled with a charred piece of brake line. "Say, look at this!" He turned a hose in his hands. "Interesting."

"Sir?" Howell moved under the vehicle.

"This brake line was tampered with."

Constable Howell craned his head to look at it from different angles. "How can you tell? The broken end is all jagged, consistent with an accident."

"Yeah, it's jagged all right, but it's not crushed. If hitting a hard object broke this, the end would be pinched. This end is jagged but still round. I saw this trick a couple of times while I worked in Toronto. To do this, you hold something hard on one side of the line, then smash it with a jagged rock. Next, you use a sharp instrument to open up the ends of the line so the brake fluid can flow. Then you glue the ends together, and the first serious braking causes the line to separate. In seconds, you have no brake fluid."

"And no brakes," Howell commented.

"You've got it."

"Whew!" Howell said. "Garret Simmons was murdered."

Meyers pulled the brake line down a little so it hung free. He motioned for a camera-carrying officer to come over. "Get a good shot of this, will you, Dirk?" He stepped back. "At least three angles." Standing fully erect, he wiped his hands on a blackened rag and spoke to Howell, "We're looking for someone who had something to gain by Simmons's death, someone with mechanical skills and the ability to get at his car." Meyers suddenly grinned. "He was a politician. There's probably a list of people a mile long who wanted him dead."

Howell pulled a notepad from his shirt pocket. "Where do we start?"

The staff sergeant carefully wiped each finger. "Where we always start. . .with the wife."

three

At six o'clock the next morning, Buck was on his horse, headed out to the pasture. Despite the brilliant sun cresting the hills in the distance, the November morning still smelled crisp with an invigorating tingle in the breeze. The heat rising from Breezy—his strawberry roan mare—along with Buck's fleece-lined jean jacket kept him comfortable. Wouldn't be long before snow would fall and he'd be hauling hay out on the tractor. There was still enough pasture for the animals to feed themselves.

Normally he wouldn't check on his two hundred head of Angus until late afternoon, but the night before, he'd heard coyotes about. He wanted to make sure his animals were all right. Buck and Breezy emerged from a forested area and entered the six-hundred forty-acre pasture. Black blobs against sky and trees, grazing cattle paused to look up, then returned to their meal, unconcerned.

Seeing nothing amiss, Buck reigned Breezy around the herd, then turned the horse toward home. A few minutes later, a dark lump in the distance caught his eye. With gentle pressure from his legs, Breezy broke into a trot. Buck moved her up into a lope. The dead body of a calf took shape as he approached. Buck bit down on his lower lip and held back a curse.

The calf was the runt of the current year's crop, the least able to defend itself. Buck looked over at his herd and shook his head at them. Why were they so dumb? They were bigger and tougher than the coyotes. Why hadn't they stuck up for their weakest member? He laughed at himself. He knew the answer, of course. The same meekness that God had put into the cattle allowed him to control the large animals and sell them to put food on people's tables.

Buck turned the horse toward home. He would come back later with the tractor and haul the carcass away so it wouldn't rot and become a source of disease. He pulled in a deep breath of fresh country air and thanked the Lord for what he owned. His parents had started the ranch, and he'd purchased it from them. Now they spent their days in sunny Arizona, and he kept on doing what he'd loved since childhood.

Loping across the wide expanse of the pasture, Buck suddenly felt a deep sense of loneliness. He was blessed beyond measure, but he had no one to share his life with. Had things unfolded as he'd planned, there would have been a son or a daughter riding beside him. This minute, Alicia would be at the house, making breakfast. Instead he was riding alone, and the only face to meet him would be the grizzled old mug of his ranch hand, Isaac McRae.

His heart ached as Alicia's face passed before him. Buck looked up at the sky, silently asking if there were any way things could be straightened out between them.

A rifle shot cracked from the direction of his home. What could Isaac possibly be shooting at? Maybe it was a bear. With a sharp squeeze of Buck's legs, Breezy broke into a gallop.

Horse and rider sailed across the field. Buck gently pulled back the reins when they got close to the wooded area that separated the house from the field. Breezy dropped down to a lope, and they worked their way through the trees. A faint, pungent odor reached Buck's nostrils. The closer they got to the house, the stronger the smell became. He'd know that stench anywhere. Isaac had nailed a skunk. Or maybe it was the other way around.

Buck and Breezy emerged from the woods and headed for the barn. Isaac stood by the chicken coop, a rifle at his side.

Buck dismounted, wrapped the reins around a hitching post, and approached Isaac. By now, the smell was enough to make his eyes water. "What happened?"

Sinewy and as lean as an old corral gate, Isaac McRae stared down at the ground, his lips pursed. He jerked his head toward the coop where the chickens crowded against the back fence, as far from the enclosure as they could get.

Gasping, Buck reached for his handkerchief to wipe his eyes.

Isaac muttered, "I saw the skunk start to dig under the wire. By the time I got outside with the .22, he'd gotten under and was in the coop."

Buck shook his head in disbelief. "You ought to know that when you kill a skunk, it releases its spray."

Isaac nodded and spat on the ground. He propped the rifle against a wooden fence rail. "I knew that since I was in short pants, I reckon."

"Why didn't you chase him out?"

"'Cause I heard once that if you shoot a skunk in the head, he don't spray."

Buck looked up at the sky as though calling down divine guidance. He stared at Isaac. "Did you shoot him in the head?"

"Nope. I missed."

Dabbing at his eyes again, Buck paused to glare at the old ranch hand. Isaac had his hands thrust deep into his overalls and looked every bit like a schoolboy caught stealing eggs. Buck suddenly broke into a loud laugh. "Isaac, sometimes I wonder about you."

Isaac shuffled his feet. "You're not the only one."

"The chickens won't be able to stay in there for at least a week. You'll have to rig up a temporary coop using one of the horse stalls."

"I'll get right on it," Isaac said, looking relieved. He picked up his rifle.

Buck slapped the old timer's back. "Let's get some breakfast. I hope it's ready."

Isaac revealed a toothy grin. "Pretty close. How about bacon, eggs, beans, and toast?"

"Great. By the way, the coyotes took down a calf last night. We might have to take turns sleeping out there for awhile. Since you've got such an itchy trigger finger, I thought maybe you'd like to. . ."

"Take the first night."

Buck smiled and gave him another slap on the back. "You got it."

After unsaddling his horse, Buck headed to the house. He entered the mudroom and kicked off his boots before entering the large country kitchen. The air was filled with the smell of bacon and eggs. . .with a tinge of skunk smell mixed in for good measure. Buck sat at the solid oak kitchen table while Isaac started to reheat the breakfast he'd put on hold when he grabbed his rifle.

"By the way, there was a call for you," Isaac said.

"When? This morning?"

"Yeah, a female."

"Really?" A touch of irony tinged Buck's voice.

Isaac chuckled. "I thought that would get you. Actually, it sounded like a young girl. Said her name was Sally and that you and she are friends. She wants you to call her back."

Buck got up from the table and went over to the phone stand. A phone number in Isaac's scrawl was on the pad with *Sally* written underneath. Why would Sally phone him? He stared at the phone. It was six-thirty. Should he call?

"She said it was important," Isaac said.

Buck picked up the receiver and punched seven buttons.

"Hello," a young girl's voice said.

"Hi, Sally. It's Buck. Is everything okay?"

"Noooo," she drew out the sound, fear in her voice.

"What's the matter, Honey?"

"It's Mommy. She won't wake up."

"What do you mean she won't wake up?"

"When I shake her, she won't wake up. Once, when I screamed right in her ear, she waved her hand and said, 'Back to bed.' Then she went to sleep again. She didn't even open her eyes, Mr. Buck. She never does that. Nobody's here but Mommy, and I'm scared."

When Sally started to cry, he knew he had to get over there. His first thought was about sleeping pills. Since Alicia did respond, even if she wasn't totally awake or coherent, he doubted she was in any danger. Still, he had to get over there, or, did he just want to get over there. *Lord, I am so confused. Please help me do the right thing, for the right reason.*

&

Ten minutes later, Buck slowed his blue Ford F250, flipped his left turn signal on, and turned off the highway onto Peterson Road. A mile down the gravel road, he turned into the long, paved driveway of the Simmons home. Garret Simmons had done well for himself. The two-story, white, colonial home was one of the best in the area. It had well-manicured lawns with expensive yard ornaments and an in-ground pool off to one side. In addition to sitting on the regional district council, Garret had been very successful with his real estate ventures.

After hopping from the truck, Buck jogged to the front door and knocked.

"Who is it?" Sally's muffled voice called from the other side.

"It's me, Buck."

He heard the dead bolt snap. Finally, the door swung open. Dressed in pink pajamas, Sally's stood before him with a stuffed toy hanging from her hand. She looked at him with a tearstained face.

"Is your mommy still asleep?"

"I don't know." Sally puckered up for another cry.

Buck touched her shoulder. "Take me to Mommy, and I'll make sure she's all right."

Sally reached out and took Buck's hand. He followed her down the hall and up the stairs. At the end of the hall, they entered Alicia's bedroom. Buck let go of Sally to kneel beside the bed. Part of his firefighter's training included first aid. Putting a lid on the panicky feeling that gripped him, Buck forced himself to calmly check Alicia.

She lay under a deep blue comforter, a pink flannel gown buttoned to her chin. Her skin was pale, cool to the touch. "Alicia?" he called, his voice strident. "Alicia, wake up!"

No response. Her breathing was deep and regular.

He leaned over and shook her shoulders hard. "Alicia!"

A scowl formed on her face. Her mouth puckered. "Leave me alone!" she muttered and tried to turn away from him.

He lifted her eyelids. The pupils dilated normally. Her pulse was slow but not slow enough to cause alarm. He looked over at Sally and gave the little girl a smile.

"Is Mommy going to die?" she asked, a new storm of tears brewing.

"Your mommy is really tired. She wants to sleep all day." Buck took a firmer hold of Alicia's shoulders and shook harder. "Alicia, you've got to wake up!" he shouted. "You've got to wake up."

She tossed her head from side to side. "Leave me alone. I'm tired."

"Mommy! Mommy!" Sally squealed. She threw herself across her mother's chest. "Wake up, Mommy!" Her words faded into shrill sobs.

Alicia shook her head but didn't open her eyes.

Buck frowned. He walked into the adjoining bathroom. Opening the medicine cabinet, he spotted a bottle of sleeping pills. Worried, he popped open the cap. The bottle was almost full. Bottle in hand, he returned to Alicia's bedside.

He gently pulled Sally off her mother and spoke very clearly, close to her ear. "Listen, Honey. She's going to be all right." He touched the child's straggly hair. "Why don't you go into the bathroom and blow your nose?"

Sally rubbed her damp face and trudged toward the open bathroom door.

With the child out of the way, he knelt beside the bed and shook Alicia hard. "How many pills did you take?" he bellowed.

She tried to roll away from him.

He pinned down one shoulder and spoke directly into her face. "Alicia, I need to know how many you took."

Forcing her eyes open, Alicia stared up at Buck. She seemed to make an effort to focus on him but failed. "What are you doing here?" she asked in a groggy voice.

"Sally called me. She couldn't wake you up. How many pills did you take?"

Alicia stared at the bottle through half-closed eyes. "Three."

"Three! You're only supposed to take one."

Her eyes drifted closed.

Sally stepped up beside him. "She's still sleeping." It was an accusation.

Buck put his arm around the child. "She's really tired. When she gets up she'll probably need some strong coffee. Why don't we go downstairs and make some?"

Sally nodded. As he walked down the hall with the little girl, he heard her stomach rumble. "When was the last time you ate?"

"Yesterday."

"Well then, I think maybe we should make you some breakfast first."

In the brightly lit kitchen, Buck dug through half a dozen maple cabinets before he managed to come up with a box of multicolored cereal and a red plastic bowl. In the side-by-side refrigerator, he found a gallon of milk. Soon Sally was happily munching away.

Buck found coffee filters and was looking for a coffee can when Sally asked, "Where's my daddy?"

Buck turned slowly. "Huh?"

"Where's Daddy?"

Buck sat at the table across from Sally. "Your daddy died, Sweetheart."

Sally nodded. "I know. But where is he now? Mrs. Dupre next door says people either go to heaven or hell when they die. Where did my daddy go?"

Buck's mouth went dry. How was he supposed to answer that question? From what he knew about Garret Simmons, he doubted the man was a Christian. Stalling for inspiration, Buck asked, "Why do you want to know?"

" 'Cause I want to go where he went," she answered, then took another spoonful of cereal.

Buck leaned back in his chair. "You don't mean you want to die too, do you?"

Sally shook her head. "I just want to be with Daddy when I die. I need to know where he went so when I die, I can tell the angel where to send me."

Buck leaned forward and took Sally's free hand. "Do you believe your daddy loved you?"

Sally nodded vigorously.

"Then, no matter where he is, where do you think he wants you to go?"

A puzzled look crossed Sally's face. "I dunno."

"Is heaven a nice place or a bad place?"

"A nice place."

"Then, no matter where your daddy is, where does he want you to be?"

"Heaven?"

"That's right," answered Buck.

Sally's spoon paused between the bowl and her mouth. "Does that mean Daddy might be in. . .you know?" Her lower lip began to tremble.

"Sally, no one knows where your daddy went except for God. He's the only One who knows what was in your daddy's heart. No one can answer your question."

Sally scrunched up her face, thinking hard. "Daddy was a nice man. I think he went to heaven. When I die, that's where I want to go."

"That's good to hear, Sally."

"So, you're starting in on my daughter now?"

Buck spun in his chair to see Alicia standing in the doorway, a thick emerald-colored bathrobe slanting off one shoulder of her flannel gown. Her hair was tangled, her eyes puffy. He'd never seen her look worse, but to him, she was beautiful. "It's not like that," he said. "She asked me where her daddy went."

Gripping the doorjamb, Alicia swayed like a wino on a binge. "I need coffee."

He stood. "Coming right up. Where do you keep it?"

"In the freezer."

Alicia disappeared into the living room while Buck dug out the coffee. In short order, he had the drip coffee maker producing a strong, dark brew. When the pot was full, he called out, "Do you like it with cream and sugar or black?"

After a moment's hesitation, a shaky voice replied, "Cream and sugar, please."

Buck brought two giant steaming mugs into the living room

where Alicia had curled up on the soft, white sofa. Buck set a large, black mug on the glass coffee table in front of Alicia and retreated to a lounge chair. He sat and felt like he'd sunk into a bowl of cotton.

Alicia sat up to reach for the coffee. Her robe was on straight now. She sipped, then looked up at him. "Buck, what are you doing here?"

"Sally phoned me. She couldn't wake you, and she was worried."

Alicia took another sip and propped her slippered feet on the coffee table. "The fight with Garret kept running through my mind. Two pills just didn't seem to do the trick, so I took one more." She touched her forehead. "I guess I should thank you for coming over."

Buck sipped coffee. Everything in him told him he ought to leave now, but something kept him glued to his chair.

Alicia's face took on more life. She stared at Buck. "Why were you preaching at my daughter? Don't you think that's a bit out of line?"

Dismayed, Buck said, "Alicia, she asked where her father went after he died. You were unconscious upstairs. What was I supposed to do?"

Fire rose in her eyes. "I suppose you told her Garret went to hell because he wasn't a Christian."

Buck set his cup on the table beside him. "I told her no one but God knows where Garret went," he said carefully.

"Well that's a change." Alicia ran a hand through her tangled curls. "You sure seemed to know where I was going back in the good old days."

He said wryly, "I've mellowed some since then."

"Am I still going to hell because I don't believe like you do?"

Buck stood. "I'd better go. The last thing I want to do is fight with you."

Alicia stared into her coffee cup. "I'm sorry, Buck. Those pills must have loosened my tongue. I don't know why I said that."

"I understand."

Tears brimmed in her eyes. "You've got no idea how horrible I feel."

"I just wish we could have done more to save him." He felt as though his throat would close up.

"You did the best you could. I know that."

A solid knock sounded at the door.

Alicia looked up at the brass clock on the mantle. "Nine o'clock. That must be my mother."

"I'll get it," Buck said, relieved to be out of a tense situation.

He strode into the hallway and pulled open the door. A tall man with white hair, coal eyes, and broad shoulders stood outside. He wore a gray trench coat over a navy suit and carried a small briefcase.

"Can I help you?" Buck asked.

The man gave him a quick once over, then flashed a badge. "I'm Staff Sergeant Larry Meyers of the Royal Canadian Mounted Police. I've come to ask Mrs. Simmons some questions. Who are you?"

Buck stiffened. "Buck Connelly. I'm with the fire department."

The sergeant nodded. "You're the man who informed Mrs. Simmons about the accident, aren't you? Why are you here?"

"I'm a family friend."

"I see. May I come in?"

"Sure," Buck said, standing aside. He led Sergeant Meyers into the living room. "Alicia, this is Staff Sergeant Meyers of the RCMP. He wants to talk to you."

Alicia set her feet down and straightened up on the sofa. "What's it about?"

"Your husband's murder, Ma'am," Meyers said, shortly.

Alicia's eyes widened. "Murder? They said it was an accident." She looked at Buck. "It was an accident, wasn't it?"

"That's what the constable said at the scene," Buck replied. His mind took off in four or five directions at once, like a bowl of spilled marbles.

Meyers set his briefcase beside the free lounge chair and sat down uninvited. "New evidence has come up. It looks like foul play. Mrs. Simmons, do you know of anyone who might have a motive to kill your husband?"

four

It wasn't lost on Meyers that Alicia Simmons was a young, attractive woman, and Buck Connelly was about her age. It struck him as odd to find the firefighter at the Simmons' home. He'd have to do some checking into Connelly.

In response to his question, Alicia Simmons stammered, "No, I can't think of anyone who would want to harm Garret." She began to tremble, and Connelly quickly moved to her side. "I just can't believe this," she said, tears flowing. "I mean. . .Garret sold real estate. Who could hate him enough to kill him?"

"That's what I hope to discover, Mrs. Simmons." Meyers looked over at Buck. "Some of the questions I have to ask will be of a personal nature."

Buck said, "I'll be going now."

Alicia Simmons grabbed Buck's arm before he had a chance to stand. "Please, stay. I don't want to be alone."

Buck lowered himself back onto the couch.

The Sergeant flipped open a black leather note pad. "Did your husband gamble?"

"No."

"Are you in financial difficulty?"

"Are you kidding?" Buck jumped in. "Look at this place."

Meyers frowned. "If you don't mind, I'd like Mrs. Simmons to answer the questions. As you should know, having things doesn't necessarily mean prosperity."

"The answer is no," Alicia said softly. "At least, I don't think so. Garret handled all the money."

Sergeant Meyers leaned forward. "I would think a real estate agent would know about life insurance. I imagine you must be set up pretty good now."

"Hey," Buck's eyes darkened. "I don't like what you're insinuating. Maybe Alicia should have a lawyer here, if these are the kinds of questions you're going to be asking."

Meyers pinned Buck under a heavy stare. "Why would she need a lawyer? You seem to be doing a pretty good job of answering all of the questions for her."

"I don't know how much insurance there is," Alicia said. "Our lawyer has all the details."

"And who would he be?" Meyers asked, jotting notes.

"Bob Kellerman."

"Would you be willing to call Bob Kellerman and authorize him to release the information to me?"

Alicia Simmons looked over at Buck. "Should I?"

He shook his head. "The way Sergeant Meyers seems to be headed, maybe you should say nothing without a lawyer."

Meyers closed his notebook and replaced it inside his jacket pocket. "Mrs. Simmons, I won't kid you. The wife is always a suspect in a murder. If you're innocent, the sooner I can clear you as a suspect, the sooner I start looking elsewhere. If I have to get court orders, it will slow me down."

Alicia Simmons stared at the floor, twisting a tissue she had in her hand. "I'll call and give him authorization."

"Good." Meyers pulled out his notebook and flipped it open again. "I understand you and your husband had a fight the day of his death."

Alicia's eyes sparked. "How did you know that?"

Buck met her gaze. "I told the constable at the scene of the accident."

Alicia stiffened, a frown appearing.

A penetrating beep sounded from Buck's belt. He snatched

his pager from its holder. "It's the fire department," he said, jumping to his feet. "I gotta go." In two seconds, he was down the hall and out the door.

Alicia Simmons watched him go, a confused expression on her puffy face. She adjusted the belt on her bathrobe and looked at Meyers, waiting.

"For what it's worth," Meyers said, "as a firefighter, he is required by law to assist the RCMP in an investigation. If the constable asked him about your state of mind when he gave you the news, he'd have to tell what he knew."

Her expression softened somewhat. "Does that mean everything I tell him, he has to tell you?"

"If he's in his capacity as a firefighter, yes. As a friend, well, I would hope he'd be honest with me, but he's under no more obligation than anyone else. Have you told him something I should know?"

Alicia shook her head. "No."

"Just how close are you and Buck Connelly?"

"We were engaged back in college."

His eyes widened. "Really?"

Alicia Simmons held up her hand. "It's not like that. Yesterday was the first time we've spoken since our breakup ten years ago. He happened to be the one responding to the 911 call for help."

"No kidding. So what did you break up over?" Meyers asked, pencil poised.

"Religion."

"Religion? I take it he's not the church-going type."

Alicia's mouth twitched. "No, it's me. While we were dating, he became one of those born-again Christian types. He said if I didn't 'accept Jesus,' he couldn't marry me."

"And what did you say?"

"I told him to get lost."

"Did you regret it?"

Alicia looked away to stare out the window. "I'd be lying if I said no." She shrugged. "We were a good match, but there was no way I'd pretend to believe in something just to get him to marry me. I figured if he loved his God more than me, he could keep Him." She peered at Meyers. "Does this have anything to do with Garret's death?"

Meyers flipped a page over and said, "Tell me about your fight with your husband yesterday."

❧

Buck pulled his pickup into the fire hall parking lot. The doors to all four bays stood open—the pumper, two tankers, and the first aid vehicle were gone. There must have been a good turnout for that call if all the vehicles had already left. Normally, Buck was one of the first to arrive, his home only a couple of miles down the highway; but with the extra distance from Alicia's place, he wasn't surprised to be last.

Buck wheeled into a parking spot, then jumped out of his still-running truck and jogged to the farthest bay where the turnout gear hung. The door to the recreation room opened. Karen stepped out and said, "Wow! I'm glad to see you!"

"What's happening?" he asked, leaning down to untie his work boots.

"It's the Stuart place. Their barn's on fire. The hay is burning. It's a real mess. The guys could sure use your help."

Buck stepped into rubber boots and pulled the straps of the protective coveralls over his shoulders. "Let them know I'm on my way." He grabbed his coat and helmet and jogged back to the pickup truck. Shifting it into gear, he sent a shower of gravel out from the back wheels. There was a loud screech as the tires left gravel and hit pavement. The powerful engine roared. The Stuart family lived close to Buck's place.

As Buck sped down the highway, he saw a thick plume of

smoke rising in the distance. He felt a new sense of urgency as the swirling gray cloud grew thicker. With that much smoke, the fire had to be a bad one.

As usual, there were cars parked along the side of the highway, everyone watching the show. Fortunately, the Stuart place was located a hundred yards off the road, so the fire trucks were able to park off the highway. Buck pulled his pickup truck onto the dirt driveway and parked about thirty feet back from the nearest tanker.

He jumped out of his pickup just as the blaring siren of the first tanker filled the air. The heavy truck lumbered away from the pumper, headed back to the hall for more water. Buck felt a strong breeze and spotted clouds forming in the distance. That's all they needed: a windstorm.

Two hay storage sheds that were each half the size of the fire station burned out of control. Flames reached out to ignite a third shed. With the sheds full of that summer's hay crop, the firefighters were in a losing battle.

Buck jogged to the control station of the pumper truck where Jeff monitored the dials and switches. Even one hundred fifty feet from the blaze, the air felt hot against Buck's face. "This is way too big for us," Buck shouted over the roar of the fire.

Jeff nodded. "We called Spruce Grove for backup, but they've got a fire of their own going right now."

Buck shielded his eyes as he watched a half a dozen volunteers battle the flames eating up the roof of the third shed. It made sense to abandon the other two sheds. They were beyond hope. He shifted his gaze to the faded house and weathered barn. "Has anyone checked to make sure no one is at home?"

Jeff glanced up from the controls. "Kurt did. House is empty."

"How about the barn?"

"Oh, man!" Jeff burst out. The shifting wind pasted bits of burning hay against the side of the barn, and the dry timber had ignited.

"We didn't have time," Jeff shouted. "The first hay shed was burning pretty good by the time we got here. We used all our efforts to try and stop the second one from catching fire."

Buck turned away. Jeff gripped his arm and yelled, "Where are you going?"

"To check out the barn. Someone may be in there."

Jeff shook his head. "I'm sure no one checked it. We barely have enough guys for the hoses."

"I'll check it then." Buck looked over the structure. The fire was still lapping at the walls. The main supports were probably untouched.

"Are you crazy?" Jeff yelled, then his voice was lost to the cackling roar of the fire.

Buck was a veteran firefighter. He'd seen a lot over the years. There was always a risk in entering a burning building, but Buck loved horses, and it sickened him to think some animals might be trapped inside the barn.

Buck grabbed an axe and trotted down toward the barn. The wind whipped pretty hard against him. He unlatched the two large doors and pulled them open. Smoke billowed out past him. *What's going on?* He could see spot fires throughout the barn floor. Debris must've blown in through an opening up top. He'd have to go back and get help. Before he turned, Buck heard stomping and neighing coming from the back of the barn. He knew fire well. By the time he got back to the truck, strapped on an air pack, the animals would be dead. There was no time. Sidestepping spot fires started from falling debris, he came to three paddocks, each with a horse trapped inside. The fire was starting to burn through the walls. Timbers above were catching. He had about two minutes to get out.

Screeching in terror now, the horses kicked their stall doors. Buck felt his way across the wood floor and came to the first stall. He unlatched it, swung the door open wide, and the horse bolted. Buck waved his hands and scared it into the direction of the open doors.

It went smoothly at the next stall. He unlatched the stall door. The grey Arab broke free from its deathtrap and fled to safety. Buck came to the last stall and groaned. The latch was padlocked. He looked up at the black quarter horse. "I'll bet you're an escape artist," he muttered. "But a padlock?" He'd run into a few horses in his time that could open almost anything, but he'd never seen a lock like this.

Buck pulled his axe from his belt and chopped away at the latch. The horse jumping with each hit. Wood splintered with each blow until the latch finally broke away. Buck swung open the door, and the horse just stood there.

"Yah!" he yelled and waved his arms. The horse backed away deeper into the stall. "I don't believe this."

It was a dumb move and went against everything he knew about horses, but Buck hated to see the beautiful animal die. He entered the stall and herded the horse until it was facing the open door.

"Yah!" He slapped the horse's rump. A hoof struck hard to his midsection. Buck doubled over and collapsed to the stall floor while the animal bolted free. Clutching his stomach, Buck sucked hard for what air there was near the ground. He lay on his back, looking up at the rafters fully ablaze and ready to come down at any moment. He rolled over, tried to get up on his hands and knees, but collapsed again. There was a loud crash as part of the roof fell to the floor. "Oh, Lord, don't let me die here, and please, don't let anyone die trying to save me."

Looking across the barn floor, Buck saw a shimmer of light against the smoke. Pulling himself forward with his elbows, he crawled toward what he hoped was an opening. He winced when a chunk of flaming wood bounced off his helmet. After ten feet, the pain in his midsection subsided enough that he could get up on all fours. Crawling like a toddler headed for a new toy, he reached the wall farthest from the fire and nearly cried with relief.

He'd come upon a partially opened manure chute. Buck pushed the door and crawled outside. Strong hands grabbed under his armpits and dragged him away from the inferno. The next moment, Buck looked up at the grim face of Rick Dupre.

"Why were you in the barn?" the chief demanded while Buck got to his feet.

"You want the truth or a good lie?" Buck asked, still gasping. He felt like his lungs were scorched.

Ignoring the feeble joke, Dupre's expression didn't change. He simply waited.

"I was rescuing the horses."

"Did you follow protocol? Did you go back for an air pack, for help?"

Buck pulled off his helmet and wiped his bleary eyes. "No time, and I couldn't stand the thought of those animals burning to death."

"I should suspend you," Dupre said, "but I won't."

Buck stared at his chief. "You won't?"

"You're not getting off easy," Dupre said. "I want you to develop an hour-long lecture for the whole crew on when not to enter a burning building."

Buck tried to stifle a grin. "Hey, no problem."

Dupre started to walk away, then turned. "Oh, yeah. For

the next eight weeks of fire practice, your job will be to wash all of the trucks, whether they need it or not. Any problem with that?"

five

Sergeant Meyers opened a solid steel door and entered the spacious waiting area of Robert E. Kellerman, Barrister, & Solicitor. The room had two white, Italian leather couches facing each other with a teak coffee table between them. Glossy magazines lay neatly on the polished wood. As Meyers walked in, an ageless secretary looked up and smiled. Her frosted hair stood out in a spiky style, and her makeup had been applied with a fine, distinctive flair.

"May I help you?" she asked. With that voice she could have been in radio.

"I'm Sergeant Larry Meyers. I believe Mr. Kellerman is expecting me."

She picked up the phone. "Please have a seat. I'll let him know you're here."

Meyers walked to the nearest wall to admire a Thomas Kincaid original in a gilded frame. A discreet cough behind him brought him around.

"Sergeant Meyers? Bob Kellerman." The lawyer extended his hand, and Meyers shook it. Kellerman wasn't at all what he had expected. He was young, thirtyish with dark, curly hair, a well-trimmed moustache, and an affable smile. He wore a hand-tailored navy suit. "Step into my office, and we'll talk," Kellerman said.

Meyers followed him down an oak-paneled hallway, passing half a dozen offices staffed by beautiful young women. Kellerman's office was at the end of the hall. Meyers took his time looking over the brass bust of Clarence Darrow on a chest-high pedestal beside the window, then he glanced at the fully outfitted bar on the left.

"Have a drink, Sergeant?" Kellerman asked, pausing by his guest.

Meyers found his voice. "No, thank you." He turned toward the lawyer. "How many partners do you have?"

"None," Kellerman replied as though amused by the question.

"Who are all those people down the hall?"

"Secretaries and paralegals." Kellerman sat in his high-backed chair. "Please, sit down." He motioned to one of the two leather armchairs in front of his massive desk.

Meyers squeezed himself into one of the chairs.

Kellerman leaned forward, his forearms resting on the desk's edge. "The easiest way to make money in the legal profession is to have someone else do the work. That's what the secretaries and paralegals are for. Partners mean sharing profits." His smile widened. "I don't like to share." He moved the glossy black pen lying on his blotter. "I'm sure you didn't come here to discuss my business affairs."

Meyers pulled out his notebook. "I need some information on the will of Garret Simmons."

Kellerman tilted his head, his eyes narrowing. "This is a bit unusual, Sergeant."

"Mrs. Simmons did phone you, didn't she?"

"Oh, yes. It's just that I'd prefer she see the will before the police do. Is it really that important?"

Meyers frowned. "I'd prefer not to say at this time."

He shifted in his chair. "Then I'd prefer not to reveal the contents of the will."

The sergeant eyed Kellerman, sizing him up. He spoke slowly. "There's a possibility he was murdered."

Kellerman's eyes flickered. "Murdered? What gives you that idea?"

"Someone cut his brake line."

The attorney rubbed his jaw. "That's shocking." He stared into the middle distance.

"Can I see the will?"

"You think the will may give you a motive?"

"That would be correct."

Kellerman opened a long drawer at the side of his desk and pulled out a multipage document. "I'll give you a copy to take with you. I can tell you that Garret Simmons left all of his worldly possessions to his wife."

"How much was he worth?"

As though he hadn't heard, Kellerman gazed out the window.

Meyers raised his voice a notch. "Mr. Kellerman, do you have any idea how much he was worth?"

Kellerman turned his attention back to the Sergeant. "Garret was my friend. We played hockey together. We golfed together. We shared business leads. I hope you'll be discreet with this information."

"If I can, I will," Meyers promised.

"Garret wasn't worth much. He wanted to be big in politics. He was always entertaining people and spending money to promote his career."

"I was at his house. It looked pretty good to me."

Kellerman shrugged. "I'm sure it did. The guy's got a great credit rating. If you dig deeper, you'll find the house has a fat mortgage. Probably everything in it came from some credit card company. Assets certainly wouldn't be a reason to kill him."

"He must have carried insurance," Sergeant Meyers said.

Kellerman cleared his throat. "If you consider seventy-five thousand dollars insurance."

He raised his eyebrows. "That's all?"

"I tried to talk him into buying more." The attorney nodded

sadly. "I told him seventy-five grand might keep Alicia going for a year after the bills were paid. Want to know what he said?"

Meyers waited.

"He said a pretty woman like Alicia would have no trouble finding someone else to take care of her." Kellerman shrugged. "He sure put her in a tight spot."

"No kidding," Meyers said. "Since you know Garret Simmons so well, any thoughts on why someone might want to kill him?"

Kellerman shook his head. "He was a good guy. I can't imagine anyone wanting him dead. Are you positive the brake line was tampered with?"

"No doubt about it."

An amplified voice from outside interrupted their conversation. Bob Kellerman got to his feet and glared out the window. "Idiots!"

"Who?" Meyers asked, standing to take a look.

"Bear Essentials."

"The environmentalist group?" Meyers stepped closer to the wide plate glass facing the street.

Across the pavement, in front of the Regional District building, a group of twenty people waved placards while a pony-tailed man wearing a faded tee shirt held a megaphone.

"What are they protesting?"

"The destruction of grizzly bear habitats," Kellerman replied. "The fools don't realize people have to eat too."

❧

Buck's muscles ached as he turned off the valve to the garden hose. He'd just finished washing down the last fire truck. He walked over to the rack where each firefighter's gear hung and pulled his feet out of heavy rubber boots. Sitting on the bench, he slowly tugged on tan cowboy boots. To his left was the door into the recreation hall. On the other side of it, all of the guys were waiting for him.

Sucking in a deep breath, he got to his feet. He pushed the door open and got hit with raucous laughter and applause. He glanced over at the chalkboard, where someone had drawn a caricature of him wearing a cape with a big H on his chest. A horse rode on his back.

"Very funny," he said to no one in particular.

A beefy man with blond hair stood up. "Hey, Buck. Don't you think you're carrying this Bible stuff a bit too far?"

"What do you mean, Chet?" Buck asked.

"You know. This helping out your neigh. . .bor stuff." Everyone laughed as he exaggerated the neigh sound to imitate a horse.

Buck headed back the way he'd come in, but a tall thin man blocked his way.

"Okay, Hank, let's hear your joke," Buck shot at him.

Hank's brow furrowed with deep concern. "Joke? Hey, I've got no joke, man. I was really worried when you went into that barn. It's good to see you alive and kicking."

"Thanks."

"When we saw Dupre show up, well. . . ," a grin formed on Hank's face, ". . .we sure thought you were all washed up."

"But it turned out it's just the fire trucks," chimed in Chet.

Another round of laughter burned Buck's ears. He shook his head and left the hall, hoots and jeers following him. As soon as he was out of sight, a grin crept over his face. He deserved everything they gave him. He'd done his fair share of ribbing when other firefighters had goofed up, and it was payback time.

He stopped at the office to pick up a stuffed mouse, the firehouse mascot, Muskie. He wanted to give one to Sally the next time he saw her. He pulled his weary frame into his truck and drove to the end of the parking lot. A turn to the right would take him home; a turn to the left would take him to Alicia Simmons's place. He turned right.

Buck drove slower than usual, his heart pulling him in the opposite direction. At home, he'd find Isaac's mediocre cooking and a lingering skunk smell. Back the other way was Alicia. Was it right for him to visit her? This morning his motives couldn't be doubted. Sally had called him. What reason could he give for dropping in on a woman who was a widow of one day? His eye caught the gray furball beside him on the seat. Of course.

He pulled to the side of the road, checked for traffic, then headed back the other way. He made his turn onto Peterson Road, then slowed the truck to a stop just before Alicia's driveway. His stomach erupted in butterflies. He shouldn't be here, and he knew it. Buck shifted the truck into gear, pulled onto the road, and barely nosed his vehicle into the end of Alicia's driveway to turn around. Two car lengths away, with Sally in hand, Alicia stood facing him.

&

Late that afternoon, Alicia had found the house oppressive and her emotions swinging—one minute tears, the next minute rage. A few friends had come over, but putting on a brave face exhausted her. Relief washed over her when they left.

Sally, blessed with youth, coped much better than Alicia. Every now and then the eight year old would burst into tears, but they wouldn't last too long. Buck's explanation of her father's final destination had given her some comfort. Too bad nothing he could say would comfort Alicia.

After the last sympathizing lady had left, Alicia found Sally lying down in her bedroom with her favorite doll, a pudgy, cloth creation named Winnie.

Alicia leaned on the doorjamb. "Wanna go for a walk, Pumpkin?"

Sally rolled over to look at her. When she spoke, she sounded like she'd been crying. "Where?"

"Just up and down the street."

Sally rubbed her stomach. "Can we eat first?"

"How about if we go for something after we finish our walk? The fridge is full of casseroles, but I can't stand to look at a casserole right now. How does a hamburger sound?"

Sally sat up and slid her legs off the edge of the bed. "Let's go."

It was starting to get dark when they stepped outside. November evenings were crisp in northern British Columbia. Alicia wore a lined jean jacket, and Sally had on her quilted coat. The fresh air lifted Alicia's spirits a little. She pulled in a cleansing breath and looked up at the first twinkling stars.

She took her daughter's hand and started down their long driveway when headlights struck her eyes. She held up a forearm as protection from the glare. *Oh, no. Not another casserole delivery.*

The lights flicked out. "I think it's Buck," Sally chimed.

Alicia squinted. What was Buck doing there?

He switched off his headlights and turned on the inside light so she could see his face. He seemed embarrassed. "Uh, I thought this might cheer Sally up a little," he stammered. He picked up a clear plastic bag containing a large gray mouse and thrust it out the window.

"Thank you," Alicia said. She ought to feel grateful, but she only felt numb. She wanted to be alone. She took the bag and handed it to Sally.

Sally pulled the mouse out of the bag and squeezed it. "He's soft. What's his name?"

"Muskie."

The child looked up at her mother. "Can Buck stay and eat with us, Mommy?"

She shook her head. "I'm sure Buck has things he has to

do besides baby-sit us," Alicia said.

Buck said, "I do need to go."

"Please stay and eat with us," Sally called, squeezing the mouse. "You can read me a story."

Uncertain, Alicia looked down at her daughter. She hadn't seen Sally so enthusiastic about anything all day. How could she say no? She turned to Buck. "Would you mind? We're not very good company right now."

He looked sheepish. "No problem."

"Why don't you come in for a bite then? The house feels so empty."

Her arm jerked as Sally jumped up and down. Alicia marveled at the resilience of a child's spirit. Sally could still enjoy the little blessings of life. Alicia felt like she'd never smile again.

Buck eased his truck down the driveway and followed them into the house. He and Sally stayed in the living room while Alicia headed toward the kitchen to pull out a container of potato salad and some fried chicken someone had brought.

"Can we eat in the living room and watch a video?" Sally called after her.

"Sure," Alicia said, relieved that Buck stayed in the living room with her daughter.

While the food heated, she peeked in on Sally and Buck. They sat close together, looking at the new book a well-meaning friend brought over that morning. With an animated voice, Buck read the story with different inflections for each character. This enthralled Sally. Alicia retreated to the kitchen and leaned against the counter. She desperately needed some grieving room, but how could she ask Buck to keep his distance, when his presence was such a help to Sally?

six

Alicia parked one foot on the bottom rail of the corral and leaned against the top rail. She slowly sipped her coffee. It was hard to believe that a year had gone by. Once again, signs of winter appeared. Grass stopped growing, and birds booked accommodations farther south. There wouldn't be many days left for outdoor riding.

On the back of Starfire, an Icelandic pony that Buck owned, Sally giggled wildly. Starfire was over twenty years old and as gentle as they came. He'd belonged to Buck's mother who didn't care for a large horse or one so small that she'd look out of place. An Icelandic fit the bill nicely.

Because Starfire was so well trained, Buck allowed Sally to control the reins herself. He stayed close by in case something went wrong. The girl's laughter was infectious, and he grinned as he watched.

In the past nine months, Buck had become a solid friend to Alicia. He'd helped keep her car in good shape and fixed the plumbing problems in her house. He cleared the lane when it snowed and took Sally for a toboggan ride afterwards.

Watching him play with her daughter, Alicia let her mind wander to long-gone days when she and Buck meant more to each other. She had no wish to raise Sally alone. Buck was the perfect man for the job except for one little issue: Alicia still wasn't a Christian.

The crisp wind swept her hair across her face, and she brushed it away. Why wasn't she a Christian? All summer, she'd had many long talks with her neighbor, Betty Dupre, a lady who always carried a little New Testament in her purse. What Betty showed her in the Bible made sense. Shortly before Easter, Alicia started sending Sally to Sunday school with Betty. When Sally arrived home, she repeated everything she'd learned that week.

What is stopping you, Alicia? she asked herself. *Nothing.*

She smiled as she watched Buck let Sally herd him about with Starfire. The horse would head toward Buck, and Buck would dodge. Sally's shrill giggles ran nonstop.

Alicia drew in a slow breath and finished her coffee. She suddenly knew what her problem was. She felt guilty.

When she accepted Garret's diamond all those years ago, she'd compromised. She said yes to his proposal for a nice home and a good man. But her heart didn't come with the deal. It had always belonged to the man dodging a nine year old on a pony. Alicia knew she'd cheated Garret, and now she felt horribly guilty about it.

A vicious circle trapped Alicia. She cheated Garret by marrying him when she didn't love him. Now she cheated herself by not accepting Christ and the forgiveness that Betty promised He would provide.

With tears in her eyes, Alicia turned away from the corral and wandered into the barn. She found a quiet place in the back of a sweet-smelling stall used to store hay. She sat on a bale and dropped her face into her hands.

"Lord Jesus," she began, "I can't carry this burden of guilt anymore. Please, take control of my life. I want to be Yours. My life is a mess. Only You can straighten it out." She prayed for a few minutes longer. When she finished, she felt a calm, relaxing feeling as though God had put His arms around her. For the first time in her life, Alicia felt at peace.

❧

"Come on, Buck!" Sally cried, "You've got to run."

Buck wiped a healthy sweat off his brow and grinned at the little girl. He'd stopped dodging the horse to watch Alicia walk away. How much longer could he stand being this close to her without telling her what was in his heart? Sure, he loved Sally, but his love for Alicia was something alive inside him that wouldn't die. Each night, he prayed that God would bring them together.

He started in motion, and Sally placed the left rein against Starfire's neck so the horse would chase him. Buck had promised God that he would never push Christ on Alicia again, and he hadn't. Now that she was free, his oath still bound him.

There were chances to share Christ with her. Every now and then, Alicia would speculate on spiritual things; but because of his oath, Buck had to bite his tongue. He'd lost her once by demanding she become what he was. He wouldn't do it again. She'd have to find the Lord her own way. He only hoped it would be soon.

Suddenly, Buck's feet sailed out from under him.

"I've got you!" Sally yelled with glee.

Buck got to his feet and grimaced at his muddy pants. He'd been thinking so hard that he forgot to watch his step. Now he was soaked. "Yeah, you've got me, Partner," he chuckled.

"Look, Mom! I caught Buck." Sally swiveled her head around. "Where's Mommy?"

"She went into the barn."

Sally pouted. "I wanted her to see me catch you."

He grabbed the reins. "Don't worry. We'll do this again."

"When?"

"In a couple of days. Starfire is pretty old. He needs some rest. Why don't we take him back to the barn and see what your mother is up to?"

"Okay."

Buck hovered over Sally and helped her off the pony. Her eyes were bright, her cheeks red. "You're getting good at riding, Honey."

"Oh, yes!"

"When you get even better, you can ride out back with me when I check on the cattle."

"Promise?" Sally jumped up and down.

"Promise."

Sally slipped her hand into his, and Buck took hold of the reins close to the bit to lead Starfire from the corral. They crossed the farmyard and entered through the barn doors. The next moment, he spotted Alicia's form near the back where the hay was stored. "Got tired of watching us, huh?"

Alicia stood up and stepped forward. She wiped her red eyes with the heels of her hands.

"You okay?" he asked.

"What's the matter, Mommy?" Sally asked running to Alicia.

Alicia smiled for the first time in months. "Nothing's wrong, Dear. Everything's right." She noticed Buck's pants. "What happened to you?"

Buck chuckled. "Your little cowgirl there cornered me, and I slipped in the mud."

She stepped close enough to him so that he smelled her light perfume and asked, "Are you free for dinner tonight?" A light shone in her hazel eyes that he hadn't seen for years.

Buck swallowed and forced his voice to sound natural. "As a matter of fact, I am."

"Good. Come by about six-thirty." Her eyes lingered on his. "We need to talk." She took Sally's hand and walked away.

Buck's gaze never left her until she got into her car and drove out of the yard. *Talk about what?* He was afraid to hope.

Two hours later, Buck stood under a warm shower spray for twenty minutes. He wanted to make sure every trace of farmyard smell was gone. Deep inside, he knew something big had happened within Alicia. He didn't dare hope, but hope he did. He couldn't forget the way her eyes had sparkled when she asked him for dinner with that lilt in her voice he remembered so well.

After stepping out of the shower, he toweled himself down good and slipped on a terry cloth robe. Next came a date with his razor, making sure he got every hint of stubble, followed by a bracing dash of aftershave, which he topped off with cologne. He headed down the hall to his bedroom. Opening his closet door, his hand automatically rested on his suit, then backed off. Instead, he opted for some casual navy slacks, a white shirt, and a comfortable beige pullover. Double-checking his hair, Buck headed for the kitchen where Isaac was working away at a plate of chili.

"Hmm, don't you smell purty," Isaac said. He turned in his seat and gave Buck the once over. "Where you going?"

"Alicia's."

"You never dressed like that to go there before."

"Never had a reason to."

Isaac rubbed his grizzled face. "Be careful, Son. She's a woman with a lot of hurt. Take it slow."

"Oh, I intend to," Buck said, pulling a soda can from the fridge. He took two sips and carried it with him to the truck. The cold evening air did nothing to dampen Buck's anticipation. He could hardly wait to find out what was up.

Parking in Alicia's driveway, he walked to her door. Hope and fear played hopscotch with his innards. What if he'd read her all wrong? No. He'd seen that look in her eyes many years before. He'd never forget what it meant.

Buck rapped on the door, then chastised himself. He forgot to bring flowers. No. He'd done the right thing. *Don't push. Isaac was right. Alicia is a fragile woman. Follow her lead. Let it happen in her time.*

The door swung open, and Buck smiled broadly. Alicia's stone face stared back.

"Hi," he said, warning sirens going off in his brain.

"You've got some nerve," she replied, her eyes blazing.

"What's the matter?"

"You killed my husband, that's what's the matter! Jeff wanted to pull him out, and you stopped him."

He felt like he'd been punched in the solar plexus. His face went numb. How did she find out? No one saw. The truck concealed him holding Jeff back.

"Don't tell me you're going to deny it," Alicia said.

"I can't," Buck whispered.

The heavy door slammed like the lid on a coffin.

seven

Alicia leaned her head on the inside of the door and let the tears flow. She couldn't get the conversation with Karen out of her mind. It ran like a bad TV commercial, again and again until she wanted to scream. She and Sally had been at the grocery store when they'd bumped into Karen at the meat counter.

"Hi there." Karen smiled.

"Hi," Alicia said. She glanced at the roasts in the case. Which one should she get for tonight?

Karen moved her cart closer and beamed at Sally. "Doing a little shopping?"

"We're having a special dinner," Sally piped up.

Karen's face showed interest. "How nice. What's the occasion?"

"Buck's coming over. Mommy says we want to make it special."

Alicia heard Buck's name and looked up. "Sally." She had that warning tone in her voice that told her daughter she'd said enough.

Karen sidled up to Alicia. "I really admire you, Alicia. You're strong enough to do the right thing. I'm not sure I could do it."

Alicia's forehead creased. She didn't like Karen's insinuating tone. "What do you mean?"

"Getting out. . .dating," Karen said, nodding.

"Buck and I haven't been dating," Alicia said. "He's a good friend to Sally and me. That's all."

Karen went on, "I think it's great how you can forgive him."

Alicia's heart rate picked up. "What are you talking about?"

"Well, I mean the way Buck stopped Jeff from going down to pull Garret out of the car before it exploded."

Alicia felt the blood drain from her face. "What?"

Karen put her hand to her mouth. "I'm so sorry, Alicia. I thought you knew." She hurried away.

Blindly feeling for the bar in front of her, Alicia had put the cart in motion. She had to get out of the store and find a place where she could breathe.

Alicia finally turned away from her front door and tried to stop her tears. The image of Buck's tormented face swam before her bleary eyes, but she pushed it out of her mind. What a fool she'd been to think that Buck Connelly was her friend.

❧

Brokenhearted, Buck turned his truck toward home. If only he had let Jeff try to save Garret Simmons. If only he'd tried to save Alicia's husband himself. Then another thought hit him. Only two people in the world knew what had happened that day—Jeff and him.

Buck pulled the truck to the side of the road to let a red sports car pass him; then he did a U-turn and headed toward Jeff's house. Five minutes later, he pulled into Jeff's short driveway and shut off the motor.

Before him stood a four-room frame house with white siding. He knocked on the door. It burst open. Jeff stood there, fumbling with his sheepskin coat while he balanced a rifle in his other hand.

Surprised, Jeff looked at him. "What's up?" he asked, shouldering into the coat.

"I need to talk to you," Buck answered, grimly.

"No time. There's a report of a grizzly hassling the Rempel's livestock. Gotta go."

"I really need to talk," Buck insisted, a little louder than before.

Jeff shrugged and kept walking. "Then come along."

Buck followed Jeff to his blue government pickup and slid into the passenger seat. He watched as Jeff mounted the rifle on the gun rack behind them. Between them—mounted in a locked bracket—was a shotgun that Jeff affectionately called the Defender. It was a powerful weapon capable of killing a grizzly with one shot. Jeff shifted the truck into gear and flipped the switches that activated the lights and sirens. In British Columbia, a conservation officer was considered a peace officer just like the RCMP, even though he dealt with animal control and hunting issues.

"What's so important that you've got to talk to me now?" Jeff asked as he swerved to pass a car.

In the glow of the dashboard, Buck watched Jeff's face. His jaw was tight, his face determined. Buck drew back. It suddenly hit him that Jeff needed to concentrate on his job right now. "Let's talk after you finish up with this call."

They pulled off the highway into a long driveway and came to a split-level stucco home nestled in a grove of birch and aspen trees. A plump, graying woman bustled out the front door. Jeff removed his rifle from the rack, then jumped out of the truck. "Mrs. Rempel? Are you having some bear trouble?"

Mrs. Rempel's round face was flushed. Trembling, she pointed behind the house to her field. "Not any more," she spat out. "It killed one of our calves and dragged it off into the woods. If Paul had been home, he could have shot it."

"He would've been in big trouble if he had," Jeff said.

Mrs. Rempel's hands landed on her hips. "What? We're supposed to watch it kill our livestock? Do you have any idea how much our cattle are worth? They're organic."

Jeff nodded. "I'm aware of the value of your cattle, Mrs.

Rempel, but when it comes to grizzlies, no one shoots them but me unless human life is in danger."

Mrs. Rempel's cheeks puffed up. "And how about our livelihood? I suppose you're just going to let this bear get away with it." She glared at him. "I heard about you. You're an animal lover."

"Not at all." Jeff shook his head. "I'm a conservation officer. My job is to protect both them and you. If this grizzly has done what you've said, I'll catch it and relocate it if I can. Otherwise, I'll shoot it."

"You'd better catch it before it eats us out of house and home!" She spun on her heels and stormed back into the house.

"You want to wait in the truck or come with me?" Jeff asked.

"What? When have you ever seen me sit in a truck?"

"Good. I hate tramping in fields alone in the dark." He walked back to the truck to remove the Defender, two flashlights, and a couple of canisters of bear spray. He handed the shotgun, a flashlight, and a canister to Buck.

Buck hefted the weighty gun and laid it in the crook of his arm, pointing down. He looked at the aerosol can. "What am I supposed to do with this?"

"Spray the bear if you can, and shoot it if you have to." Jeff chuckled. "I don't love them that much."

Buck aimed the flashlight at the can's label. "This stuff really work?"

Jeff nodded. "That is one powerful mixture of pepper and mace. It's strong enough to kill a human under the right conditions, so make sure you don't spray into the wind."

"Gotcha." Buck glanced at the can again and shoved it into his jacket pocket.

Jeff slipped a wooden box out of his pocket and opened it. Inside lay a row of tranquilizer darts. "Mind you, if I can, I'd rather put the bear to sleep." He loaded a dart into his rifle.

The two men trudged into the field behind the Rempel home, scanning the ground, on high alert for any sign of movement. The moon shone brightly enough for them to make out the forms of cattle and trees. Buck had lived in the country long enough to know that a grizzly would track a human. Bears rarely attacked people, but when they did, it was messy.

As they approached, the Angus cattle nervously moved about. Soon the two men came across a patch of blood in the meadow grass.

"The bear must have hauled the calf off to bury it somewhere," Jeff said. "The blood trail should make it easy to track."

Half an hour later, a light mist started to settle over the field, obscuring their vision. Buck asked, "Shouldn't we come back in the morning?"

Jeff rubbed his chin and looked toward the dark woods. "If we wait until morning, the bear will be long gone. Either get him now, or Mrs. Rempel will be dragging me back out here in a week or so when the bear comes around for seconds." He glanced toward Buck. "If you're not up to it, we can go back."

Buck wasn't up to it. He wanted to go home and lick his wounds, but he wasn't about to admit that to Jeff. "No, I'm all right. Let's go."

Jeff licked his finger and held it in the air. "Good thing there's not much breeze tonight. At least he won't be able to smell us coming."

The cattle behind them lowed and started to shuffle. Buck glanced back at them. "Boy, they're still pretty spooked."

"Can you blame them?"

Since the mist hadn't quite settled on the ground, they could follow the blood trail with a flashlight. "Why would a grizzly go after a calf?" Buck asked. "I thought they liked berries and fish."

"They do," Jeff said. "Unfortunately, so much of their habitat has been destroyed, there aren't many berries available. Because of overfishing, the river doesn't have the stocks it used to. They're like any creature—they'll do whatever it takes to survive."

They trudged toward a swath of trees that surrounded the Rempel farm. "How are things going with Alicia?"

With the hunt for the bear, Buck had almost forgotten his anger, but it flared at Alicia's name. He stopped in his tracks. Every word grew louder than the one before it. "It was going fine until you opened up your big, fat mouth."

"What are you talking about?" Jeff turned to face him, his eyes wide and glistening in the dim light, a mixture of surprise and fear.

Before Buck could answer, a deep, guttural snort sounded behind them.

❧

At her tiny kitchen table, Alicia grabbed for another tissue. "He killed my husband, Betty! All these years, he's been pining away for me. He saw his chance, and he took it."

Slim and graceful with her red hair in a casual, sweeping cut, Betty Dupre patted Alicia's hand. "Oh, Honey, I'm sure that's not what happened. That's not Buck. If there'd been any way to save Garret, Buck would have done it. My husband is the chief, and he told me that Buck was acting according to protocol when he stopped Jeff from going down that hill to Garret's car."

"Buck couldn't deny that he let Garret die," Alicia sobbed. "All this time, he's been weaseling into our hearts. I just can't believe this."

Betty put her arms around Alicia.

Alicia pulled back a bit. "You know what makes it even worse?" She pressed a tissue to her eyes.

"What?"

"I accepted Christ just hours before I found this out," Alicia said. "I thought God took away our burdens. This isn't quite the deal I thought it would be."

With concern in her eyes, Betty Dupre watched Alicia and gently said, "God takes away every burden except the ones we want to carry."

Alicia sat up and glanced at Betty. "Well, I sure don't want to carry this one."

Betty smiled. "I'm sure Buck didn't do anything wrong, Alicia."

Alicia jumped to her feet. "How do I explain to Sally that the man she's come to adore let her father burn to death? He's got to pay for what he did. My little girl will never be the same." She scuttled to the phone table, opened the drawer, and found a business card. Lifting the receiver, she punched in a number.

"Sergeant Meyers? It's Alicia Simmons. I'm sorry to bother you at home, but you said I should call if anything ever came up. Well, something has come up."

&

The air exploded from Buck's lungs. Fire seared his back, and he flew head over heels onto the wet grass. His face plowed into a clump of stiff timothy. By sheer instinct, he rolled sharply to the left, and the grizzly skidded past him. It spun around for another attack. The Defender lay on the ground ten feet out of reach. Through his peripheral vision, Buck watched Jeff raise his rifle and fire, but the dart whistled over the bear's head.

"Play dead!" Jeff yelled, circling around.

That advice went against everything in Buck. A wild animal was trying to kill him, and all he could do was stay still and hope the beast thought he was dead. He wanted to fight back, but he knew that no one ever won a fight with a grizzly. Tucking his knees against his chest, Buck put his hands over his neck and curled into a ball.

The bear gave him a healthy swat. Buck's ribs exploded in pain. He gritted his teeth and held back the urge to scream. From the corner of his eye, he could see the dark form of Jeff moving for The Defender. The grizzly spun on its haunches and chased Jeff away. The creature had no idea Jeff was going for the gun; it just saw him as competition for its prey.

"Close your eyes and mouth. Pinch your nose. Whatever you do, don't breathe!" yelled Jeff.

Buck clenched his eyes and mouth shut. He pinched his nose until it almost split in two. The bear gave him another swat, and he tumbled like a beach ball. Then came a *swooshing* sound, and pepper bear spray hit him. The animal snorted in anger but backed away. More spray shot over his head, and the bear howled again. There was a loud explosion, and Buck knew the bear was history.

"Don't open your eyes!" Jeff shouted.

It was too late. Buck's eyes were on fire. He gasped, and his lungs caught the flame.

He groaned in agony. Over his moans he heard Jeff say, "Thank God."

Cool water flooded Buck's face. Through blurred vision, he could see the stout form of Mrs. Rempel standing over him with a glinting metal pail in her hands.

"I was watching from the house," she said. "Don't ask me why, but when I seen the grizzly break out from the herd, I just knew you'd have to use the spray, so I grabbed a bucket of water and came a'running."

Buck tried to thank her, but only a deep moan came out.

Jeff shined the flashlight on his face. "Man, I better get you to the hospital." He reached for his cell phone.

๛

Sitting on his worn living room sofa with the telephone pressed to his ear, Meyers listened as Alicia Simmons told her story. Reaching for the remote, he turned off the hockey game and asked, "You're saying that Buck stopped Jeff Thompson from rescuing your husband?"

"That's right," Alicia said into the phone.

"Why am I hearing about this now? We've been digging for over a year, and there hasn't been a whisper of this."

"Buck and Jeff have been friends since grade school," Alicia said. "They're tighter than brothers. Buck probably told Jeff to keep his mouth shut. I don't think we ever would have found out if Karen hadn't spilled the beans."

"I've often wondered about that situation. Do you realize that Buck Connelly, just after Garret's accident, went into a burning barn alone to rescue some horses? I feel certain that his feelings for you affected his actions at the accident scene. I've felt it all along."

"Can you do anything?" Alicia asked.

"I'll head out to his place first thing in the morning and bring him in for questioning. With this new evidence, we just might be able to crack the case."

eight

Larry Meyers pulled his police cruiser into the long driveway that led to Buck Connelly's home. He'd heard rumors that the farmers who'd switched to organic beef were doing well, and Connelly's home supported that belief. It was a nice three-level split with aluminum siding and a steel roof. The barn in the back was wood frame, painted red with white trim.

He parked the car near the side door and eased his large frame outside. Sucking in a deep breath of country morning air, he let out a satisfied sigh. He liked breathing air he couldn't see. If he could talk his wife into it, he'd move to the country in a flash.

"Can I help you?" A gruff voice spoke behind him.

Larry Meyers turned to face a man about five foot eight, dressed in overalls, with three days of stubble on his face. He was walking over from a nearby chicken coop.

"I'm Sergeant Larry Meyers of the RCMP." He flipped open his badge. "I'm looking for Buck Connelly. Who would you be?"

"Isaac McRae. I'm Buck's farmhand." The older man peered at the identification, then looked at Meyers's face as if to make sure he really was the man in the photograph. "Buck ain't here right now."

"Oh, any idea where he is?"

The old farmhand chewed on his bottom lip. "Why do you want to know?"

"I'd rather discuss my reasons with Mr. Connelly himself."

"I suppose it'd be all right to tell you. He's in the hospital."

Meyers lifted his eyebrows. "The hospital?"

"Yeah. Got attacked by a grizzly last night."

"How bad is he?"

McRae shrugged. "Not too bad. His buddy, Jeff, managed to kill the griz."

This wasn't something Meyers had expected. "I guess I'll have to see him there, then." He glanced at the neat yard, the house, the barn. "Do you mind if I look around the place a bit?"

McRae stiffened. "What for?"

"I'm from Toronto, originally. I don't know much about farms. This is my first chance to have a good look at one. Would you mind giving me a tour?"

McRae's sullen expression brightened by half. "Sure. The more you city folk understand what we do out here, the less troubles we'll have."

"Troubles?"

"We've got a booming market for our beef because no one in this whole valley uses any chemicals or pesticides. We feed our cattle nothing but grass and organic grains. Now the only way we can expand is to remove the timber on the government land behind our farms for pasture, but we can't because the city folk keep writing letters, and the provincial government won't give permission to cut the trees."

"Is there really that much money in organic beef?"

Isaac McRae hitched his thumbs into his suspenders. "It gets better every year. With the mad cow disease scare in Europe and the fear of genetically modified foods, people are looking for food they can trust. In this valley, we can produce it. We ship beef all the way to California."

Meyers looked the farmhand over. Isaac McRae appeared to be a simple farmer, but he seemed to have a good grasp of the market. "That's fascinating," Meyers said. He looked toward the barn. "So, how about a tour?"

For the next half hour, McRae led him around the farm. It all looked pretty good, but the shop got Larry Meyers's attention. A hydraulic hoist for lifting vehicles stood in the middle, and tools covered the walls.

"Does every farmer have a shop like this?"

McRae shook his head. "Nah. Buck studied mechanics in college. He's pretty handy with tools. He likes to fix all his own stuff."

"What kind of stuff?"

"The tractors, farm implements, the trucks."

"Like pickup trucks?"

"Sure," McRae said. "Oil changes, plugs, brakes."

Meyers looked at his watch. "Thank you for your time, Mr. McRae. I've got to be moving along. I'll visit Mr. Connelly in the hospital."

❧

Trying to sit up in his hospital bed, Buck grimaced. He felt like he'd spent the previous day riding bulls, and the bulls won. His ribs hurt when he breathed in, and his throat felt raw. He took a sip of cool water from the jug beside the bed. It helped some. After swinging his feet over the edge of the bed, he slipped into the hospital-issue slippers and found his way into the washroom. He looked in the mirror and saw his red, puffy eyes. He'd never touched a drop of liquor in his life, but the bear spray made him look like a thirty-year heavy drinker.

His face was nothing compared to how he felt inside. All night, Alicia's face flooded his dreams, always within his grasp, but somehow he could never reach her. Last night, he tried to punch Jeff right there in the ambulance when Jeff admitted he'd told Karen about the incident at Garret's accident scene. The burly ambulance attendant held Buck down.

Sore from the bear attack, Buck couldn't fight back. Yesterday would go down as the worst day in his life. They couldn't come any worse than this. He had two dozen bruises, fifteen stitches behind his left shoulder, five more in his arm, and the mother of all headaches besides.

Moving in slow motion, he shuffled back into the bedroom and started digging his clothes out of the closet. He'd wanted to go home last night, but the doctor insisted he stay in case he developed breathing problems. Earlier this morning, a different doctor—the one on call—had given him the green light to go home.

He slipped off the hospital gown and put his feet in both pants legs when he heard the door open. He yanked up his jeans and turned to see Sergeant Meyers's large frame filling the doorway.

"Hello, Buck," the sergeant said, stepping inside. "I need to ask you a few questions." He let the door close behind him.

Buck slipped on his shirt and reached for the top button. "What's on your mind, Sergeant?"

"Why did you stop Jeff Thompson from saving Garret Simmons's life?"

Buck rubbed his chin. "So Karen didn't think ruining my relationship with Alicia was enough. She had to call you in."

Meyers's eyebrows arched. "Karen?"

Buck cocked his head sideways. "Karen Russell. The woman who gave you your information."

Meyers shook his head. "It wasn't Ms. Russell, Buck. I can't tell you who it was." He moved closer. "Is it true? Did you stop Jeff?"

Buck stared at the floor. Alicia had called Meyers. "Yeah," Buck answered, finally. "It's true."

"You physically prevented Jeff Thompson from trying to rescue Garret Simmons?"

"There was a power line on top of the car. It was too dangerous."

Meyers's eyes narrowed. "You felt it was unsafe?"

Buck burst out, "It's against protocol to approach a wire."

"Wasn't it unsafe in 100 Mile House?"

Buck looked up at Meyers. "How did you know about that?"

Meyers reached for his notebook. "I've done some checking up on you, Buck. You're quite a hero, quite a risk taker, except when it came to saving the life of Garret Simmons. Could that have anything to do with the fact you've been in love with his wife for years?"

"Of course not!" Buck's chest tightened. He was having breathing problems after all.

Meyers nodded, his mouth set. "Sure it didn't. Tell me, just when did you tamper with Garret's brakes?"

Buck did a double take. "What are you talking about?"

"Garret Simmons's brakes were cut. Your farmhand tells me you know all about brakes. When did you sneak over there and cut the lines?"

Buck went to the closet for his jacket. "This is too ridiculous to talk about."

Meyers crossed the floor and towered over him. "Not as ridiculous as killing a man to be with his wife. Make it easy on yourself. Tell me the truth."

Buck swallowed and realized that his hands were trembling. On top of the bear attack this was too much. "The truth? The truth is I was scared. Since 100 Mile House, I've been terrified of power lines."

"Then why didn't you let Thompson go down the ravine?" the sergeant asked. "He wasn't scared."

Buck said, "If something happened to him, I knew I didn't have the guts to go after him."

Meyers smirked. "You had the guts to save some horses from a burning barn. Too bad Simmons wasn't a horse." He stared at Buck, his eyes hard and dark. "Where were you the night before Simmons's car crashed?"

Buck looked into Meyers's face. Hostility was written all over it. "I think maybe I should talk to my lawyer."

Meyers nodded. "That would be a good idea. You can call him from the station." He produced a pair of handcuffs. "Buck Connelly, I am placing you under arrest for the murder of Garret Simmons. You have the right to remain silent. You have the right. . ."

Meyers's words drifted off in an echo. Buck couldn't believe what he was hearing. He was under arrest for murder? He'd been wrong. There could be worse days ahead.

⌘

In a spare, but clean, office, Larry Meyers sat across the wide oak desk from Crown Prosecutor Arthur Dunfield. A lanky lawyer with fine features, Dunfield tapped his bony fingers on the page before him while he read the file on the Simmons murder. When he finished, he pursed his thin lips together and looked at the sergeant.

"This is all you've got?" the prosecutor asked.

Meyers nodded. "Isn't it enough? Means, motive, opportunity—they're all there. He has no alibi for the night before. He could've sneaked to the Simmons' home and messed with the brakes."

Dunfield rubbed his chin. "It's all circumstantial. You have nothing physical to connect him with the crime like fingerprints or fibers."

Meyers held his hands out, palm up. "The car burned up. There was precious little physical evidence."

Dunfield sucked in his bottom lip. "You honestly want me to prosecute a local hero based on circumstantial evidence?

Do you realize we have to convince the jury beyond a reasonable doubt that he did this? The first thing a defense lawyer is going to ask is, 'Why did he wait ten long years to do it? Why didn't he kill the guy when he was good and mad?'"

He threw the file to the desktop. "I don't see premeditated murder here at all. The best you might get him for is criminal negligence causing Simmons's death because he prevented the other firefighter from affecting a rescue. Even then, it's doubtful." He looked at his watch. "Where is Connelly now?"

"He's at the station in lockup."

Dunfield's eyes widened. "You arrested him on this evidence?" He pushed the file farther toward Meyers.

"I wanted to shake him up," Meyers said. "I figured some time in jail might make him more talkative. If you charge him, we could move him to the prison and work on him some more."

"Let him go. Without physical evidence, there isn't a hope of a conviction."

Meyers gave him a sour look. "And what do I tell the widow?"

"Tell her to sue him civilly," Dunfield said. "If all I had to do is prove on the balance of probabilities that Connelly let Garret Simmons die, I'd stand a decent chance of winning."

"It's not the same as putting him in jail."

The prosecutor held out his hands in exasperation. "There's nothing I can do with what you've got."

"Then I'll have to keep digging," Meyers said. He scooped up the file and stalked out the door.

⊷

After being released from police custody later that afternoon, Buck grinned weakly at Isaac when he crawled into his pickup truck. From behind the steering wheel, Isaac watched his careful, painful movements. "Bad day?"

"How about nuclear holocaust day?" Buck replied, grimacing as his shoulder came in contact with the seat. "The cops think I killed Garret Simmons."

Isaac's brow lowered. He glared at Buck. "What would make them think that?"

Buck turned away. He didn't answer.

"What's the matter, Buck?" Isaac put the truck in gear and headed for the highway.

"How's this for a fairy tale?" Buck told the story of Garret's accident again, including every pain-filled detail. Then he went on to Karen's telling Alicia about it. "Can you imagine Karen doing something like this?" Buck demanded. "Look at the trouble she's got me in!"

Isaac rubbed his gnarled hand over his grizzled face. "The way I see it, whether she meant to or not, she saved you. Did you think something like this would stay a secret forever? What if you had of married Alicia Simmons and this came out years later? What then? The woman would be your wife, and Sally would be your daughter when they found out. That would have been a nuclear holocaust day. By forcing it into the light, Karen has done you a favor. This needs to be dealt with now—not later, when it's too late."

Buck made an impatient grunt. "I think it's already too late. Alicia hates me. Karen wants to ruin me. The cops are trying to pin a murder charge on me. I'll be lucky to escape with my freedom, never mind anything else." He eased his aching back. "Why me?"

Isaac sent him a hard glance. "Son, I hope you're not feeling sorry for yourself. You've got no right to. Right now, Alicia is sitting at home, trying to deal with what she's found out. It's obvious Karen never got over you, and bitterness is eating away at her. And what about little Sally? She's become pretty close to you, and suddenly, you're gone. I think both those women and that little girl might be asking the same question. This mess is your making. You're the one to blame. You should've told Alicia what happened at the accident scene right off."

"I meant to," Buck said. "But she was so upset, I just couldn't. I figured I'd wait until later, when she wasn't so fragile. Later came, and no time seemed right."

"And things turned out better this way?" Isaac shook his head.

Suddenly, Buck sighed and slumped against the window. He stared straight ahead, unmoving, for the next three miles. Finally, he glanced at Isaac. "Yeah. . .you're right. But what do I do now?"

Isaac shrugged. "I don't know, Son. When it comes to matters of the heart, I've chosen bachelorhood, so I don't have a lot of first-hand experience. What I do know is there's a great big God up there Who understands everything, and if anyone has the wisdom to pull this off, He does. You need to do some praying and a whole lot of listening."

Buck nodded. "You're probably right."

"I know I am," Isaac said. He pulled off the road and stopped on a wide shoulder. "Bow your head, and we'll take this to the Lord right now."

Buck looked up. "Here? In public?"

"Jesus was crucified in public. We ought to be able to pray in a pickup truck."

Buck bowed and listened while Isaac made a petition to God. Although his farmhand's words were soothing to the soul, Buck had no illusions. Things would probably get worse before they got better. He hadn't done much praying lately. He'd do what Isaac said. Let God work it out.

nine

Alicia handed Betty Dupre a mug of herbal tea and sat beside her on the couch.

"How are you doing?" the older woman asked. Betty had been a good friend all through the time after Garret's death and now, through this news about Buck.

"I cried all night," Alicia said. "I feel so. . .lonely. Betrayed."

Betty took a sip of the tea. "I'd hoped that a good night's sleep would make you feel a little better."

Ready tears sprang to Alicia's eyes. "I thought Buck was honorable and trustworthy. How could he do such an awful thing?"

Betty reached over and placed a hand on hers. "According to my husband, Buck was acting according to protocol."

Alicia snatched her hand away. "Buck never let protocol stop him before or since, so why was it a reason for his actions that day? It doesn't make sense, Betty, unless you take one thing into consideration."

"What's that?"

Her voice grew vehement. "Garret was my husband. That's enough."

"Alicia, Buck would never—"

"I'm sorry, Betty, but I can't believe that anymore." Deep down, in a far corner of her heart, a little voice whispered that Betty was right. But that wasn't the voice Alicia wanted to hear right now. She was hurting too much.

"Why be so obvious about it?" Betty went on. "If he wanted to kill Garret, why now, and why in the open?"

Alicia shivered. Her arms wrapped tightly around her middle. "I don't know."

"Alicia, did you really give your heart to Jesus before this happened?"

She nodded, and her chin stayed low on her neck.

"Why did you do it?"

She shrugged. "Because it was the right thing to do, I guess."

Betty shook her head. "It has to be something more than that. When people come to Christ as adults, it's usually because some need has driven them to Him. Some crisis. What was your crisis, Alicia?"

Alicia got up from the couch, walked to the window, and looked at the rain pouring in the front yard. She knew the answer. She just didn't want to say it out loud.

Betty moved up behind her and put a hand on her shoulder. "What was it, Alicia?"

She waited a moment longer, then answered. "I realized that I was only hurting myself by not accepting Jesus. It's my soul that will be affected. No one else's. Besides that, it was the last barrier between Buck and me," she whispered.

"How so?"

Alicia faced the older woman. "During our senior year in high school, Buck became a Christian. Shortly afterwards, he came to me and gave me an ultimatum—either I became a Christian, or we had to break up. We'd been going together for four years, and boom, it was just like that. We were finished if I didn't believe like he did."

Betty gave Alicia's shoulder a gentle squeeze. "You weren't about to be pushed into something you didn't believe just to suit him."

She nodded. "I was furious. I had no idea what he believed, or why, but I wasn't going to jump just because he whistled."

"So what then? You broke up?"

"Sort of," Alicia said. "After that, he would preach at me every day, telling me my soul was in danger, and I told him if we truly loved each other, it wouldn't matter. He said he loved God more and had to obey Him. That was it. He was gone."

Betty shook her head. "Poor Buck. He fell into the trap a lot of new Christians do. They want those they love to believe, but they don't want to give God the time to work in their loved ones' hearts." She paused, then went on. "Have you considered. . ."

"I wonder what he wants," Alicia interrupted Betty as Sergeant Meyers's car pulled into the driveway. "Maybe we can finish this tomorrow."

"Sure." Betty moved to the couch to pick up her coat and canvas shoulder bag.

There was a firm knock at the door. When Alicia opened it, Sergeant Meyers blurted out, "I need to speak with you." He drew up short when he saw Betty standing behind Alicia.

"I'm going," Betty said.

"Come on in, Sergeant." Alicia pulled the door fully open.

He stepped into the hallway and bent down to unlace his soggy shoes. Betty slipped into her brown loafers and gave Alicia a hug. "Talk to you tomorrow?"

"Yes," Alicia said. "Thanks for coming over."

After Betty scurried out into the downpour, Sergeant Meyers handed Alicia his dripping trench coat. She hung it on the clothes tree behind the door and led him into the living room. Meyers sat in a lounge chair across from the couch.

"Some tea, Sergeant?"

"No, thanks," he replied. "I won't be long. I just wanted to tell you what's been happening in the investigation."

Alicia sat down. She plucked at the jean fabric around her knees. "You've got something?"

"I arrested Buck Connelly."

Alicia's heart lurched. In a way, she was glad, but immediately behind that feeling came a slow dread. She clenched her hands together and waited for him to go on.

The sergeant frowned. "I had to let him go. I have a good circumstantial case. Buck had a motive: his obsession with you. I talked to Karen Russell today, and I'm convinced he's never stopped thinking of you. I've also learned that he had the means to pull this off. He's got a complete shop over at his farm, and he knows about brakes." He shrugged. "But the crown prosecutor refused to formally charge him."

"Why not?" Alicia asked, watching the officer's craggy face.

"In a criminal case, we have to prove guilt beyond a reasonable doubt. We don't have any physical evidence, like fingerprints, tying him to the murder. There were no witnesses. The prosecutor feels no judge or jury would send Buck to prison based on what we have. Unless something more comes up, I can't go any further with this." He stood. "I'm sorry, Mrs. Simmons. I know you need closure about this. I wish there were more I could do."

Alicia drew in a slow breath, thinking. She almost felt relieved. But then bitterness swelled up. How could Buck stand there and watch Garret die? Confused and angry, she blurted out, "He has to pay for what he did, Sergeant. He let Sally's daddy die."

"I can't give you legal advice, Mrs. Simmons. I suggest you talk to your lawyer. He may be able to help you."

"I think I'll do that."

❧

Buck turned down the speed of his windshield wipers. The heavy rain was easing off. His pager blared, and the dispatcher's voice came across the truck's speaker. "We have a barn fire three miles south of Muskrat Creek fire hall. All units respond immediately." Buck pulled his truck to the side of the highway, waited for traffic to pass, then left a crescent of rubber as he headed back toward the fire hall. Sure enough, he got stuck behind an old beat-up sedan and lost precious seconds waiting for a safe area to pass. Why the government wouldn't allow volunteers to have emergency lights on their vehicles, he'd never understood. Lives depended on their fast response.

He turned right off the highway and ground to a stop in the gravel parking lot of the hall. There were already half a dozen members there in various stages of preparedness. The pumper and tanker trucks were outside their bays, waiting to take off. Buck jumped from his truck and jogged into the open doors of the truck bays.

When Buck got to his place beside Jeff, his friend was pulling on his coat. They exchanged glances but not words. Buck had been pretty hard on Jeff, but time had changed his anger to remorse. He realized Jeff hadn't meant any harm. As soon as they got a chance, he'd patch things up.

Buck noticed that everyone was ready to roll but him. "You guys get going," he said to Jeff. "I'll follow in the rescue truck."

Jeff nodded but still said nothing. He kept his face turned away.

While Buck finished putting on his gear, the two heavy trucks pulled out of the lot, lights and sirens blaring. Two minutes later, Buck hopped into a smaller rescue truck that held their first aid gear and extra breathing equipment. Emergency lights and siren on, he pulled out of the fire hall and surged down the highway. He picked up the mike to the two-way radio to double check the location. The farm was close to the last fire and near his own ranch.

When Buck pulled off the highway and into the farmyard, the members already had the hoses out and the water going.

The barn was a lost cause. It was fully engulfed in flames. All attention centered on the house. The rain had been blown away by a strong wind that flung chunks of burning debris toward the two-story farmhouse. The tar shingles were aflame, and the fire had probably already burned through to the attic. Smoke streamed out of a partially-opened upstairs window.

Two drenched teenage girls stood behind the trucks, holding their horses' bridles and sobbing uncontrollably. One of them pointed toward the house and cried. "My grandparents are in there."

Two men were on each of the hoses. One man stood beside the truck to control the water flow. Jeff was busy strapping on breathing gear, getting ready for a rescue attempt. It was wrong for Jeff to go in alone. Buck was still pretty battered up over the bear attack, but he was the most experienced member. He jogged over to Jeff. "Where do you think you're going?"

Jeff glanced at him and returned to his equipment. "I'm going in."

"Then I'm coming with you."

Jeff stood impatiently waiting while Buck strapped on his breathing apparatus. Together, they advanced toward the house, axes in hand and ropes slung over their shoulders. Flames licked out of the upper windows. Buck tapped Jeff on the shoulder and pointed toward the visible fire. His partner nodded back. They'd have to move fast.

Normally, they'd vent the house to prevent against a back draft, but there was no time. They'd have to take their chances. Buck touched the door. It was only warm, a good sign. He indicated to Jeff to stand clear in case he was wrong. The handle resisted when he turned on it. It was an older door, a good solid wooden door with a dead bolt lock.

He and Jeff jammed the pry bar ends of their axes above

and below the dead bolt. Buck's shoulder grumbled but otherwise held up. They wrenched the door open with one mighty
thrust. When they stepped into the house, light smoke filled
the lower area. It was time to make a decision. Every second
would matter. If they searched the downstairs, and the
elderly couple was upstairs, the time spent searching would
mean their death. But if the victims were downstairs, and the
firefighters went upstairs, they'd needlessly endanger their
own lives. After the last few days, Buck didn't care much for
his life. He'd leave the decision to Jeff.

Buck pointed up the stairs, then pointed at the floor and
lifted his hands in a question. Jeff pointed upstairs. If more
volunteers had shown up, they could have had two men follow
them in with a hose; but it was a weekday and most members
had jobs in town, so they made do with what they had.

The staircase was narrow and creaked under their weight.
So far, all they'd encountered was smoke billowing up
against the ceiling. When they got to the top of the stairs,
the smoke reached the floor. It was going to be a blind
search. Both men got down on all fours and crawled, reaching out with their hands, hoping to make contact with a
body—hopefully a live body.

They went directly to the end of the hall where fire peeked
through the ceiling. There was a door to each side. It was
against the rules, but with the flames so close, chances had to
be taken. Jeff took the door to the right, and Buck moved to
the left.

Buck reached up, turned the door handle, and pushed it
open. He crawled in and closed the door behind him. Through
the smoke he saw the light of the window. He walked over and
smashed out the glass with his axe. The smoke billowed out,
and the room cleared enough so he could see. It was a small
bedroom with a single bed, feminine furniture, and pictures of

teenage bands on the wall. It must belong to one of the girls outside.

He quickly checked under the bed and crossed to the closet. When he flung the door open, flames flashed out and slammed him. They flowed over his head and right out the open window. Back draft! How he hated it. The flames had eaten through the closet ceiling. All they needed was more air to continue their rampage. His equipment protected him from serious harm, but his heart thudded so hard, it hurt. Maybe he cared about living more than he'd thought.

His radio crackled. "I found them," Jeff's voice said.

Buck lunged to the bedroom door. He got low, pulled it open, and more flames shot overhead. The fire had burned through the hallway ceiling and was now making its way down the walls. He charged through the flames and yanked open the other bedroom door. No problem with back draft now. The flames were finding plenty of air from the other room's open window. He entered the room and slammed the door behind him. The smoke was light in the other bedroom, because Jeff had already torn out the window.

Jeff was bent over a thin white-haired woman lying on the floor, checking her vitals. He nodded toward the adjoining bathroom. "Look in there."

Buck crossed the room and groaned when he got into the bathroom. In a tub of water lay an unconscious, bearded man who had to weigh at least two hundred and fifty pounds.

Buck pulled off his glove and checked the man's carotid artery. There was a pulse, so Buck was spared giving him CPR. But how to get him out? No fireman was going to be able to sling this guy over his shoulder and carry him down a ladder.

He reached under the naked man and pulled out the plug. The bath water made a churning gurgle in the pipe. Buck returned to the bedroom and stuck his head out the window. Three more members had arrived. They were placing a ladder against the house. He turned to Jeff. "We're almost ready to go."

Jeff's fingers went to the woman's neck. He looked up, anguish on his face. "Her heart stopped," he said. He locked his hands and did some chest compressions. A firefighter's helmet appeared at the window. "We're ready to go, guys."

It was Chet. Big, powerful, Chet.

"You get in here," Buck said to Chet. The burly fireman didn't ask questions. He pulled his frame through the window.

"Okay, Jeff, take her out," Buck said.

"I gotta keep doing CPR," he said.

Buck's voice grew sharp. "Her best chance is the ambulance. Now get on the ladder, and we'll load her onto your shoulder!"

Jeff scrambled out the window. Chet scooped the woman up like she was a feather. Buck tied her hands together. They eased her out the window and slipped her arms around Jeff's neck. With the grandmother hanging over his back, Jeff carefully moved down the metal rungs.

As the first flames broke through the bedroom door, Buck turned to Chet. "We've got a tough job," he said, "and we don't have much time."

He led Chet into the bathroom. "Oh, man!" Chet groaned. "What're we going to do with him?"

"Let's sling a rope under his arms and lower him out the window. If you've got a better idea, I'm willing to listen."

Chet grabbed a limp, rubbery arm. "Let's move!"

Buck's shoulder shot darts of pain right into his head when he yanked on the man. He clenched his teeth, fighting through the agony. Together, they dragged the man out of the tub and into the bedroom. The door was a roaring sheet of fire. Flames from the hallway tried to decide where to go next. It wouldn't be long before they'd prefer the air coming from the window that was the firemen's only way of escape.

Jeff's head popped into the window. He stepped over the sill.

Because the man was naked, he was hard to work with. Clothes were much easier to grab. Buck pulled a blanket off the bed, and they rolled the farmer into it. They tied a rope tightly under his arms. Using another blanket as a makeshift stretcher, they were able to lift the man up to the window and get his legs out. Jeff dragged while Buck pushed, and Chet held onto the rope. They took a full minute getting his body out the window.

The muscles in Chet's neck stood out. His face grew purple. "I can't hold him!" he yelled into the helmet's mike. Buck grabbed the rope, his shoulder a throbbing mess. Together they lowered the man to the ground. What a relief when he finally touched down.

The flames raced across the ceiling over their heads. "Go ahead," Buck shouted to Chet.

Chet scrambled out the window. One second later, Buck followed. He looked up to see flames leap out the window and into the air. Scurrying down the ladder, he jogged away from the house and collapsed at the side of the fire truck. He whipped off his helmet to gulp in smoke-laced air. A short, husky paramedic appeared and placed an oxygen mask over his face. Buck took in deep draws of oxygen. He couldn't get enough cool, clean breaths.

Working with speed from long practice, the paramedic helped him pull off his coat. He checked Buck over. "Your vitals are good, but you should go into the hospital for a checkup."

Buck shrugged. He had no intention of going. He didn't like his last stay in the hospital. Jeff walked over and collapsed beside him.

"How are the old folks doing?" Buck asked him as the paramedic moved to Jeff, oxygen canister in hand.

Jeff drew in a long breath, then lifted the mask to say, "The woman's going to be all right. They shocked her and got her heart going. The husband's awake in the ambulance. He's pretty shook up." He lowered the mask and breathed.

Buck glanced at the barn. "It seems pretty odd that the barn would catch fire during a downpour. What do you think?"

Jeff shook his head and lifted the mask again. This time he took it off. "Thanks, Mark," he told the paramedic. "I'm okay." When the medical officer trudged away, Jeff turned to Buck. "We've got an arsonist on our hands, Buck. Last time, he only burned up a hay crop. This time, he almost took two lives in addition to the hay. I hope the cops catch the guy before he kills someone."

"Me too."

Jeff lightly punched Buck's arm. "I'm sorry about earlier on."

"About what?"

"About being such a jerk. I had other things on my mind." He looked troubled. "I got a phone call from Karen. She doesn't want to see me anymore. She won't say why."

ten

Waiting in Bob Kellerman's plush anteroom, Alicia fidgeted with the handle of her burgundy handbag. Several business, sports, and news magazines lay on the table before her. She glanced through them and laid them down. Nothing could hold her attention for more than three minutes these days.

With little else to do, Alicia gazed out the window at Kellerman's small parking lot. The beautiful morning sky had clouded over, and rain was beginning to fall. Was this some kind of message from God? Was He warning her that she was about to make a mistake? No. She doubted God would change the weather just to get her attention. For two weeks, Alicia had wrestled with the decision. Should she see her lawyer or not? Last week, when Sally had another nightmare about her daddy, Alicia decided to call Kellerman. But the next morning, she couldn't make herself pick up the phone. What if Betty was right and Buck hadn't done anything wrong?

The dilemma was solved for her when Bob Kellerman phoned the previous day. He'd read the police report and wanted to talk to her. He said it was important.

Her attorney walked into the reception area, a broad smile on his face. He extended his hand. "I'm sorry to keep you waiting,"

Alicia stood and shook his hand. His grip was gentle. After holding her hand a couple of seconds longer than normal, he released it and touched her elbow. "Come into my office."

At the door, he paused to let her enter first. She'd known

Bob since high school. He'd been charming then, and he seemed to have improved with age.

By the window stood a large oak desk with two seats in front of it. He motioned her to the left where a coffee table stood between two red leather love seats. On the coffee table lay a solitary manila file folder.

"Why don't we sit over here?" he asked and pointed to the love seats. "It's much more comfortable."

"Sure." Alicia chose the love seat with its back to the wall and sank into its deep softness.

Kellerman went to his desk and picked up his phone, his finger hovering over a button. "Would you like something to drink? Coffee, tea, juice?"

"Coffee would be nice," Alicia said.

"How do you like it?"

"Cream and sugar."

He punched the button. "Two coffees," he said. "Cream and sugar in both."

The lawyer sat across from her and smiled. "How are you doing?" Sincere concern on his face, he waited for her to answer.

Alicia twisted her hands and looked down. "Not bad."

"You look good," he said, "except for those dark circles under your eyes. Have you been sleeping?"

She looked up at him. "Things have been pretty tough. Sally keeps begging me to ask Buck over, and I haven't found a way to tell her why he doesn't come around anymore."

Kellerman nodded. "I can imagine how difficult this is for you."

The door opened, and the receptionist carried in a tray. On it were two ceramic mugs of steaming hot coffee and a selection of pastries. With a wide smile for her boss, she left the room and closed the door.

Alicia picked up the coffee and took a sip. Bob's words were casual and friendly, but there was something more in his eyes that she didn't want to deal with right now.

He picked up the file folder and leaned back in his seat. "This is the reason I insisted you come in. I've read the police report, and I believe that Buck Connelly killed your husband."

Alicia felt a jolt. To hear Kellerman say it made it seem so. . .real. She saw Buck's slow grin and heard his deep voice murmur her name. Could the same man really be capable of murder?

"I also agree that a criminal court would never convict him. The evidence is all circumstantial." He put the folder down and leaned toward her. "However, I think he will be found guilty in a civil court. I think you ought to sue him." He lifted his mug and took a sip.

Avoiding his eyes, Alicia looked out the rain-streaked window. She didn't want to face a lawsuit. Seeing Buck in the defendant's chair would be torture. "I'm not sure I should." She turned to face Kellerman.

He set down his cup. "I don't think you have a choice."

"What do you mean?"

He took her hand, squeezed gently, and smiled. "Alicia, people are going to find out what happened. There are going to be questions. . .and rumors. They'll ask, 'Why didn't she sue him?' People will think maybe you had a part in it."

Alicia pulled her hand away. "That's ridiculous."

Kellerman sat back in the loveseat, arms wide on the back of the seat. "Is it? The man let your husband die, and you do nothing. People are going to think that at the very least, you still love him." His eyes sought hers. "Do you?"

"No." Alicia said it too quickly and too loudly. She looked away.

Kellerman sighed. "Well, if not for your reputation, you

should at least sue him for the money. Garret didn't leave you much. You've got to face it. After all the bills were paid, you've got enough money to keep you going for maybe another two or three months, but then you're going to have to get a job. You'll probably have to move into the city and put Sally into after-school day care. Is that what you want?"

Alicia shook her head. "Of course not." Sally loved the country, and putting her in day care was unthinkable. "I can't afford to pay you to represent me."

Kellerman reached for her hand again. "You don't have to pay me. I'll work for a contingency fee. I get forty percent of whatever we win, plus disbursements. If you get nothing, I get nothing."

Alicia slowly shook her head, a doubtful expression on her face. "I don't know. I mean, we'd be wiping Buck out. I'm not. . ."

"Oh, don't worry about Connelly. He's insured through the fire hall. He won't pay—his insurance company will. This is a win-win situation. You get the money you deserve to take care of Sally, and Connelly will have to take moral responsibility for Garret's death. Only the insurance company has to pay any money."

Alicia stared at the deep navy carpet. She suddenly wanted to cry. Garret had been burned so badly that the casket had to be sealed. She hadn't even gotten one last glimpse of him. Maybe she should let the courts decide if Buck was guilty.

"Okay," she whispered.

"Great." Kellerman pulled a document out of the folder and set it on the table. With one smooth movement he took a pen out of his shirt pocket. "Sign here, and I'll get the ball rolling."

"That fast?"

Kellerman grinned. "I had the documents prepared earlier. I know this is difficult for you, so I wanted to make sure you didn't have to come back in to sign paperwork. I'll take everything from here."

※

In the cluttered study of Buck's ranch house, he clicked the mouse, and another Web page opened. "Did you talk to Karen?" he asked Jeff, who was watching over his shoulder, a coffee cup in hand.

"Unfortunately, I did."

Buck glanced over his shoulder. Jeff's face was haggard, his eyes puffy. Whoever said men didn't cry hadn't met them. Buck had spilled plenty of tears into his pillow, thinking about how he'd lost Alicia again. He couldn't let himself think about Sally. He loved that little girl like she was his own. Every minute of the day, he agonized over the pain he'd caused her.

"She give you a reason for breaking up?" Buck probed.

"You'll never believe it. She's still in love with you."

Buck felt like he'd been kicked in the ribs. He rubbed a weary hand across his face. "I'm sorry, Partner."

Jeff shrugged. "I am and I'm not. I'm glad to have found out now instead of later. It's going to hurt for awhile, but I'm sure God has someone else out there for me."

Buck nodded and turned his attention back to the computer. The land titles records of the Province of British Columbia appeared on the screen. "Okay," he said, a trace of excitement in his voice. "Let's see what we can find here."

He typed in the legal description of the farm where the first fire had been located and waited for the page to load. "Well, well," he said a moment later.

Jeff took a seat beside him. "It's been sold to a numbered company," he read. His expression tensed. "I never thought the Carmichaels would leave this area."

"Me neither," Buck said. He typed in the legal description

of the second fire. Both men whistled in unison. "Sold to a different numbered company," Buck murmured.

"This certainly looks suspicious. Looks like someone is burning them out so they can pick the places up cheap. How much were the properties purchased for?"

Buck's fingers danced on the keyboard. He shrugged when the numbers appeared. "Both prices are about right. Maybe even a little on the high side. This doesn't make sense. Why torch the barns, then pay fair market value?"

Jeff stood up and paced around Buck's study. "Without a good reason, those people wouldn't take fair market value. They loved farming."

Buck swiveled in his desk chair. "With their barns and hay gone, why not sell? Considering the time it takes for the insurance money to come through and the time to build new barns and replace the hay. . ."

"They'd have to sell all their livestock and start over again next year," Jeff finished.

"So by burning them out, someone gets their property. But for what?"

Jeff sat down again. "That I don't know. With the current zoning policies and the restriction on expanding, these properties aren't that valuable. The only thing they've got in common is that they border the timber zone on this side of the highway."

"They're fairly close together," Buck told him.

Jeff pointed to the computer. "I don't suppose you can make that thing tell us who owns those numbered companies?"

Buck nodded. "I think so." His fingers moved on the keyboard, and another Web page appeared for corporate records. He punched in the numbered companies. After a few moments, he sagged in his chair. "Figures."

Jeff looked at the screen. "Both companies are owned by a

trust in the Cayman Islands. Welcome to the end of the road."

Buck pushed his chair away from the computer and slapped his knee. "Whoever owns those companies burned out our neighbors. They may have only meant to take out their barns and hay, but they nearly killed the Jameses, not to mention the Carmichael's horses. There's gotta be a way to find out who they are."

"I'll give this information to the RCMP," Jeff said. "It's their job to investigate arson anyway."

Buck leaned toward the computer and touched the screen. "I'd sure like to know what's so valuable about those properties. I wonder if some zoning change is planned, if someone has inside information."

"I'm sure the police will look into that."

A knock at the door echoed down the hallway.

"I'll have to get that. It's Isaac's day off." Buck got up from the computer and walked down the hallway. He opened the front door to the pouring rain. A woman barely over five feet tall stood there, smiling sweetly. "Buck Connelly?"

"Yes," he answered. He looked over her head to see if anyone was with her. What was she doing all the way out here?

Her right hand appeared with an envelope in it. She placed it against his chest.

"You've been served." She spun on her heels and scampered to a beat-up economy car, shielding her hair from the rain with her hands.

The envelope dropped to his feet. Buck bent over and picked it up. Closing the door, he stared at the envelope like it was a rattler about to strike. Just when he'd started thinking his troubles were passing, more trouble met him at the door. Holding the envelope slightly ahead of him, he shuffled down the hallway.

When he entered the study, Jeff looked up. "What's that?"

Without answering, Buck slumped into an easy chair in the corner and tore the envelope open. He gazed at the legal document for a full minute.

"What is it?" Jeff asked.

"Alicia is suing me for two million dollars for the wrongful death of Garret Simmons."

❧

Alicia took a sip of hot chocolate. The rain hadn't let up all day, and the air felt damp. Sally was upstairs reading a book, so Alicia was enjoying the peace and quiet. She still felt a little troubled over the lawsuit, but Bob Kellerman was probably right. Buck let Garret die, and she had a daughter to support. Besides, the insurance would pay.

She picked up a magazine and idly flipped through the pages, sizing up some hairstyles. Maybe it was time for a change. Maybe even a different color. A tall brunette with a striking perm caught her eye when the doorbell rang. She set the magazine aside and went to the door.

Opening the door, she sucked in a short breath. Buck stood there, drenched. His denim shirt clung to his skin. His dark hair lay glued to his head. He held up his hand to show her a soaked piece of paper.

"What's this all about, Alicia? Why are you doing this?"

Alicia tried to close the door, but he blocked it with his foot.

"Why, Alicia?" he demanded louder.

Her jaw tightened. "Buck, anything you have to say, you can say to my lawyer."

He brushed water from his dripping face. "I didn't kill Garret. I love you too much to hurt you that way."

Alicia took a trembling breath. Her voice grew shrill. "Please go away," she begged.

"Not until you hear me out! I didn't want Garret to die. I had my reasons for stopping Jeff."

Alicia had enough. She tried to close the door again, but he still held it back. Finally, she screamed at him. "You stood and watched Garret die!"

Suddenly, Buck looked shocked. He wasn't looking at her anymore. He was looking past her. Alicia turned. Sally stood in the hallway, the stuffed mouse tucked under her arm.

"You killed my daddy?" The mouse dropped to the floor. Sally's face crinkled. Her lower lip trembled. Alicia turned and scooped Sally up in her arms. "Why did he kill Daddy? I thought he liked us."

"I. . .do," Buck stammered.

Alicia whirled around. "Get out of here! Haven't you done enough?"

He stood there like a statue. "But. . .Sally needs to know. . . ."

"There's nothing she needs to hear from you! Go! Now!" She slammed the door with all her might, then carried Sally into the living room and set her down on the couch.

"Did he really do it, Mommy?" her daughter asked, eyes wide, her lips frowning.

Alicia sat beside her. "There's something you need to hear, Honey."

She told Sally all she knew about what had happened at the accident scene. She told how Buck had never stopped loving her, and that's why he might have let Daddy die. Listening intently for ten minutes, Sally watched her face.

When Alicia finished, Sally shook her head. "If Buck loves you that much, he didn't let Daddy die."

"How can you know that?" This wasn't the response she'd expected.

"In Sunday school, we learned that love always wants the best for someone else. If Buck loved you, letting Daddy die wouldn't be the best for us. He didn't mean to, Mommy.

Buck's a nice man. He'd never hurt Daddy." She climbed into her mother's lap.

Alicia held Sally tightly to her heart. She felt as though she were an actor in an old spy movie where the ceiling was dropping slowly down, smothering her.

eleven

Buck pushed open the glass door of Clarence Brown's office and stepped into the tiny reception area. Half a dozen cloth-backed chairs lined a corner section of the room with a square table filling in the corner. The receptionist looked like the ink on her business school diploma was hardly dry. Her long fingers were a blur over the keyboard. Turning a page of the material she was typing, she must have sensed Buck's presence, because she glanced up, smiled, and brushed a long strand of cinnamon-colored hair from her face. "Can I help you?" She had a soft, lilting voice.

"I'm Buck Connelly. I've got an appointment with Clarence."

She scanned the open appointment calendar beside her and nodded. "Yes. He's just on the phone right now. If you'd like to take a seat?"

"Sure."

The young woman flashed him another smile and went back to her computer. Buck found a seat near the magazines. His stomach was in knots. He couldn't stand the thought of facing Alicia in court. He picked up a fishing magazine and laid it back down. Clarence was an attorney who loved to fish. He and Buck had pulled in quite a few trout together. They went way back, and Buck knew his friend would steer him in the right path.

Three doors stood behind the young lady's desk. The center one opened. Tall and lean, Clarence Brown stepped out of his office. He was dressed in a charcoal suit, and he wore his dark hair slicked back. He sure looked different at work than he did fishing. At the office, he was strictly professional. On the lake, it was blue jeans, fishing vests, and plenty of bug spray.

His face formed the easy grin that came from meeting a good friend. "Buck, it's good to see you." They shook hands. "Come on in." He stood aside to let Buck pass into his office.

Buck chose the left chair in front of an expansive walnut desk. From the fifth floor of the office building, they had a nice view of Prince George.

Clarence paused inside the door. "Coffee?"

"Sure," Buck replied, turning in the seat.

Clarence disappeared into the reception area and returned shortly with two Styrofoam cups.

"Doesn't your receptionist do that?"

Clarence grinned. "She's got lots to do." He kicked the door shut. "Sure is a nice-looking girl, isn't she?"

Buck looked at a framed photograph on the desk— Clarence's wife and two sons. Moving around the desk, the lawyer noticed Buck's interest in the picture. His smile widened. "Don't worry, Buck. I hired her because she's an excellent legal secretary."

"Uh-huh," Buck said, taking his cup.

"And she's my niece." Clarence chuckled as though he'd just told a great joke. "She's new to town, you know, and not seeing anyone. Just in case you're interested."

"Once burnt, twice shy," Buck said.

Sinking into his chair, Clarence shook his head. "Hey, Buck, don't let this lawsuit make you a lifetime bachelor. Paula's a levelheaded girl. She'd make any guy a fine wife. It looks to me like you tied up with a nutcase when you got involved with that Simmons woman."

Buck's face stiffened. "Don't talk about her that way."

Watching his client carefully, Clarence leaned back in his

chair. "You still care about her." It was a statement of fact.

Buck nodded. "Guilty." His voice was full of misery and regret. He set down his cup. "But even if I didn't, she's not a nutcase. She's been through more pain than any woman should face, and I'm afraid I caused it."

Clarence picked up a file and glanced in it. "Are you admitting that you let her husband die?"

"Not for a minute," Buck retorted. He pointed to the file. "What's that?"

"It's the case against you. The law requires Bob Kellerman to give me everything he's got and vice versa. I've already read through it." He slapped the file to the table. "To be honest, Buck, they've got a good case. I kind of hoped the coroner's report would have indicated Garret Simmons would have died from his injuries, but it's clear, if not for the fire, he would have lived. He could have been saved.

"Now, personally, I wouldn't believe for a minute that you'd let a man die. Unfortunately, what your friends believe doesn't count. The judge will decide the issue. Based on this, they've got an eighty percent chance of winning."

Buck rubbed his clammy hands on his jeans. This was the last thing he wanted to hear. "Maybe I should settle."

Clarence shook his head. "Absolutely not." He picked up a silver pen from the blotter. "Besides, it's not your decision."

"What do you mean it's not my decision?" Buck leaned forward in his seat. "I'm the one who's being sued."

"I'm afraid it's not that simple. The fire hall's insurance company will have to pay any damages. In fact, if you were to admit guilt, the insurance company would have a good reason to deny the claim. You must say nothing to anyone about this case except to me and the insurance company's lawyers."

"When do I meet with them?"

"Probably in a couple of days," Clarence told him. "I'm going to send them a copy of this file. They'll have a look at it and make an appointment to meet with you. From that point on, I'll have nothing to do with the case anymore."

Buck cocked his head sideways. "You mean I don't even get to pick my own lawyer?"

"I'm sorry, Buck. This is their ball game. They have to write the check, so they get to make the rules." Clarence smiled, trying to soften the blow. "In a way, it's a good thing."

"How so?"

"Mrs. Simmons needs money. This way, you can help her out, and it costs you nothing."

Buck wasn't buying it. "What about my reputation?"

Clarence shrugged. "It's already smeared, Buck. Rumors will do more damage than a trial ever could. At least with a trial, you get your side of the story in the open."

Buck scowled. "You didn't make my day. I hope you know that."

Clarence spoke seriously. "You really should take my niece out. You need a new lease on life."

Buck held up his hand. "Listen, if I want to try something new, I'll buy a boat and go to West Lake."

Clarence glanced at his watch. "Look, it's lunchtime. I've got to stay here and finish a couple of briefs. Brighten Paula's day and take her to lunch. As a favor to me."

Still adamant, Buck shook his head no.

"Great." Clarence picked up his phone. "Paula, my friend, Buck, wants to treat you to lunch. He's a great guy, and he has horses, so I don't want to hear no." He dropped the receiver and grinned.

Buck exhaled sharply and glared. "What are you doing?"

Clarence grinned, all his teeth showing. "She's a great girl. You'll like her."

"I'm sure she is, but. . ."

"You can't back out now and hurt her feelings." Clarence stood. "Come on, I'll introduce you."

Buck forced himself out of his chair and followed Clarence. What an insane thing for Clarence to do. Buck had visions of their next fishing trip and some *nice* surprises he could spring on Good Friend Clarence—sand in his lunch bag, a nice cold dip in the river. . . . They stepped out of the office and into the reception area.

"Paula, this is an old friend, Buck Connelly," Clarence said.

Paula looked up. She smiled, uncertain. "Hi."

Clarence slapped him on the shoulder. "I gotta get back to work," he said and disappeared into his office. He closed the door behind him.

"It's okay if you don't want to take me to lunch. My uncle is always trying to fix me up." Paula sounded painfully insecure. He'd figured that such a pretty woman would have the guys lined up at the door, but now he suspected that wasn't the case. She shuffled some papers on her desk.

Buck truly didn't feel like taking a girl to lunch, but it was never in his nature to hurt anyone's feelings. "I admit your uncle can be pushy, but I hate to eat alone, and I'd really appreciate your company."

Her soft brown eyes lit up. A smile spread across her face. "I'll grab my things." Placing one hand on the desk in front of her, she pushed herself to her feet in a definite, awkward motion. As she walked over to the coat rack, her left leg moved slower than the right. It clicked with each step. She lifted her jacket and turned around. She noticed him looking at the leg of her green slacks.

"That's why I never wear a dress."

When he didn't answer right away, her jaw tightened. "Uncle

Clarence didn't tell you I have an artificial leg, did he?"

Buck's face grew hot. He didn't like being caught off guard. "No, he didn't."

She hung the jacket back on the rack. "You don't have to go to lunch with me. I'll call across the street for a sandwich."

"Why wouldn't I?" Buck asked, finally back on track.

"Because I'm a cripple." The words sounded brittle.

Buck grinned. "You're a very attractive woman. I'd be honored to take you to lunch." He moved closer to her. "I'm a cripple too."

She glanced at his strong hands, then at his cowboy boots. "No, you're not."

"I've only got half a brain. Otherwise, I wouldn't be in this lawsuit."

She laughed and grabbed her jacket. He held open the glass door, and Paula passed through. They waited for the elevator, and moments later, they were out on Third Avenue, the sidewalks busy with lunchtime pedestrian traffic.

"What kind of food do you like?" Buck asked, dodging a waist-high boy who ran by.

"All kinds," Paula said. "You choose."

"There's a great steak place half a block from here."

"Let's go," she said. "I'm starving."

They started up the street at a moderate pace. The weather was mild, and they had a nice stroll to the Cariboo Grill. When they stepped through the door, the warm aroma of grilling beef wrapped around them. The dining room had a western flavor with red carpet and a buffet. The place was moderately busy. Booths lined the walls, and tables filled the center. A pleasant-faced woman wearing a red shirt and a black skirt seated them at a booth by a plate-glass window that overlooked the sidewalk.

Buck glanced at the menu, but he already knew what he'd

order. Paula's eyes darted back and forth across the laminated card. "What are you having?"

"Steak and baked potato. I'm not very creative when it comes to food."

She closed her menu. "That sounds like a winner to me."

The waitress came and took their orders. An awkward silence lingered for a full minute. Paula glanced around the restaurant as though preoccupied. Listening to the gentle hum of conversation around him, Buck knew it was up to him to start talking.

"Clarence says you're new to town," he said, diving in.

"Yes." Her roving gaze rested on him. "I moved up from Vancouver last month."

"Vancouver?" he asked, surprised. "Why did you move here from Vancouver? Everyone here wants to go there. We don't get much oncoming traffic."

She shrugged. "After I graduated, I couldn't find a job. Besides, even with my pension, it's hard to get a decent apartment in Vancouver on a legal secretary's salary. Housing is so much cheaper here." For a moment, she looked out the window at people passing by. "And I guess I needed a fresh start."

"Pension?" Buck asked. "You don't look old enough for a pension. What did you do, opt for the sixty-two-year-old plan instead of waiting until you're sixty-five?"

She giggled. "It's for my leg."

The waitress brought their drinks and silverware, then hurried away.

Paula swept her hair behind her ear and tore the wrapper from her straw. "I wasn't always a legal secretary. I used to be in the RCMP."

Buck whistled softly. "No kidding. You look so. . ."

"Uncoplike?" she asked, smiling. She had a gorgeous smile.

"Yeah, and young." Buck sipped his cola.

She nodded. "I don't look like a cop or twenty-six years old. That's what made me so useful. They recruited me into narcotics right out of the academy. I worked undercover on the international drug trade for the next four years. When the time came to make the arrests, bullets started flying. I took one in the knee."

Buck looked at her as though seeing her for the first time. "How come this was never in the media? You'd think something like this would've gotten a lot of coverage."

"I was shot in the Cayman Islands where no one knew my identity—not even the drug dealers. The brass decided that I should disappear into the sunset."

Buck had a new thought. "Did you say the Cayman Islands?"

"White sand, lush hotels, and lots of money," she said. "Our team worked hand-in-hand with all sorts of agencies— the CIA, DEA, Interpol, and local officials. I was there to find a money-laundering link between a couple of Canadian banks and offshore banks on the island. Initially, we didn't intend to make the arrests in the Cayman's, but—for reasons I won't go into—our hand was forced."

Buck frowned. "Why would your leg injury keep you from being in the RCMP? Surely there was a desk job you could do. You're doing it here, aren't you?"

Paula said softly, "Once I'd tasted the thrill of being an undercover officer, I couldn't stand to sit behind a desk and watch my old team members work the field. It would have been like twisting the knife." She took a sip of ice water. "It was better for me to make a complete change. It was fun while it lasted. I've been everywhere—Europe, all through the U.S., Mexico, Barbados."

Suddenly, she reached across the table and touched Buck's arm. "You know what I'd really like to do?" she asked, her eyes dancing.

"What?"

"Ride a horse."

Buck's face crinkled. This girl was full of surprises. He'd been off balance since Clarence left him in the waiting room with her. Paula's expression reminded him of little Sally when she sat on Starfire. The next instant, the sparkle died. Instead he saw pain.

"What's the matter?"

"How can I learn to ride with this bum leg?"

Buck leaned both forearms on the wooden table and spoke gently, "With the right horse, you'd have no problem at all. I could teach you." He glanced up as the door of the restaurant opened. The next moment, his mouth went dry. He drew away from Paula.

Paula turned in her chair to see what had upset him. She glanced at him. "That's her, isn't it?"

Lips tight, Buck nodded.

"She's beautiful."

"Yeah," he whispered. He turned his glass in his hands, staring at the condensation dripping down the side, then looked up at Paula. Her face was filled with concern.

"How awful to be in love with the woman who's suing you. I'm so sorry."

"Is it that obvious?" he asked, one side of his mouth twisted in.

That moment a tall, athletic-looking man stepped in the door and took Alicia's arm. She dazzled him with a smile. Everyone in the room disappeared to Buck except Alicia. It was as if the whole universe revolved around her, and he was in some kind of personal torture. All he could do was watch and never have.

"Does this mean you won't teach me to ride?" Paula asked, teasing.

"Huh?" Buck stared at her, trying to resurface.

Paula laughed lightly. "Wow, you do have it bad."

He shook his head, still confused. "Sorry. What did you say?"

"I asked if you'd still teach me to ride."

Buck focused on Paula's face and tried to force Alicia from his mind. "Anytime. I've got a pony that's as gentle as a lamb."

⁂

Alicia let Bob Kellerman escort her to the corner of the dining room to a table beside a wall with a small wagon wheel attached to it. After he helped her take off her coat, she slid into the booth, and he slid in across from her. He'd surprised her with this offer of lunch. At first she'd refused, but when he mentioned that it was about the case, she accepted. Besides, with Sally at school, all she did was mope about and feel miserable. She had little to do with her time.

"Thank you for joining me," Bob Kellerman said, showing his perfect smile.

Alicia's lips automatically curved upward, but her heart wasn't in it.

"So, how are you doing?"

Alicia tilted her head to the right, then back to center. "Pretty good, I guess."

Bob Kellerman set his elbow on the table, cupped his chin in his hand, and stared at her. "You look sad to me."

Alicia nodded slightly. "I'm still in shock over all of this."

He sat back, totally at ease. "That's the good thing about a court case. It acts like a catharsis. Helps get everything in the open, so it can heal."

"I hope so," Alicia said, "because I still feel terrible about suing Buck."

Kellerman nodded. "Most victims feel that way."

Alicia lifted her eyebrows. "Victims?"

He reached across the table to cover her hand. She let him leave his hand there.

"Alicia, you are a victim. Buck is responsible for all of this, and he's the one who should be feeling bad instead of you."

"Then why do I feel like such a rat?"

He squeezed her hand. "You need to get out more. You're an attractive woman, and a respectable amount of time has passed since Garret's death. You don't want to be alone forever, do you?"

Alicia looked into his eyes. They were warm pools of compassion. She'd always thought of lawyers as stuffy, humorless men. Bob Kellerman was anything but stuffy. "I don't know. After Buck. . ."

Bob said gently, "Alicia, don't let Buck rob you of everything. He was a bad experience, that's all. Let him go and learn to love again. Learn to love someone else." He held her gaze for a long moment.

Alicia's cheeks burned. Suddenly, the large dining room felt like it was closing in on her. "I. . .uh. . .have to go to the ladies' room," she said, reaching for her purse.

He released her hand. Alicia clutched her handbag and headed toward the front of the restaurant. People were a blur as she rushed past them.

Thankfully, the place was empty. She splashed cold water on her face and took a moment to freshen her makeup. Snapping her compact closed, she drew in a few slow breaths. Did she feel this way because she was attracted to Bob, or because something told her to run? The only way to know for sure was to head back to the table.

Whispering a prayer for help, she started down the aisle, but a waitress with a heavy tray blocked her path. Alicia cut to the right and froze in her tracks. There was Buck, staring directly at her, his mouth half open, ready to speak. She looked at the woman across from him, a girl with gorgeous red hair cascading down to her shoulders. The woman turned and smiled at Alicia. She could have been a fashion model or a movie star. Maybe she was.

Alicia nodded curtly and headed back to Bob. A little breathless, she slid into the booth.

"Everything okay?" He seemed pleased about something.

"Absolutely," she said, forcing cheerfulness into her voice. She gave Kellerman a reckless smile. Buck was not going to spoil her afternoon out. So what if he was having lunch with an attractive woman? What was that to her?

twelve

A few days later, Buck swept the brush down Starfire's back while Paula looked on. The pony hadn't been ridden since the last time Sally had been there. Buck's throat tightened, and he made a conscious effort to steer his thoughts in another direction.

Looking sharp in a pair of blue jeans, cowboy boots, and light blue western shirt, Paula leaned against the white rail fence of the outdoor arena.

"How did you convince Clarence to give you Monday morning off?"

"It's my regular morning off. Clarence likes to use Monday mornings to catch up on his reading, so he goes to the law library at the courthouse. He locks the door, hangs out a sign, and lets the answering service get the messages. I usually end up working more than eight hours a day the rest of the week, so it balances out."

Buck bore down hard with the brush to loosen some crusted mud mixed into Starfire's hair.

"Want me to do that?"

Buck stopped brushing and noticed the hopeful look on her face. "Sure."

Paula limped across the hard-packed earth.

"You don't have to do the whole coat," Buck told her. "Brush here along his back and under the belly by his legs. All we want to do is make sure there's nothing sharp caught in the hair where the saddle is going to rest."

Paula stroked the pony's neck. Beaming, she took the

brush from Buck. He left her and went into the tack room. He opened the bag of horse cookies and dropped half a dozen into his shirt pocket. Lifting a black Wintek saddle by the horn, he got a saddle blanket and stepped back into the cool morning air. He grinned when he saw Paula vigorously brushing Starfire's legs.

"That'll be good enough for now," he said.

Paula turned around. She swept her cinnamon-colored hair from her face. Her cheeks were pink. "That was fun. I don't mind doing the rest of him."

Buck grinned. "You can groom the rest of Starfire after you finish the ride. He'll enjoy it. It's like a massage to a horse." He swung the saddle onto a sawhorse and carried the blanket to her. Turning it over, he exposed the underside. "Before you put a horse blanket on," he said, "always check the bottom of it to make sure there's nothing sharp on it such as a burr. The last thing you want is something sharp between you and the horse's back."

He rubbed his hand across the blanket. Paula did likewise, their hands touching for a brief moment. "It seems to be fine," he said. He threw the blanket across Starfire's back and saddled up.

Paula stood back, a hand on one hip, sizing up Starfire. The confidence she had while brushing the pony seemed to evaporate now that the moment of truth had arrived.

"You were an undercover cop, right?"

She nodded.

"In that case, you've been in lots of situations more frightening than riding a horse."

She looked doubtful. "Yeah, but in those situations, I always had a gun."

Buck chuckled. "Starfire is very gentle. He won't hurt you."

Paula arched her eyebrows. "Starfire?"

Buck looked at the pony. His head hung low, his tail swished gently. Buck chuckled. "His name doesn't quite fit him, does it?"

"Not exactly," she said, smiling a little.

"Then get on."

Paula limped to the pony. She glanced down at her leg. "Is it okay to mount from the right side?"

"Absolutely," Buck told her. "A lot of people train their horses to mount from the left side, and I used to be one of them until Jeff taught me different. I've trained Starfire to be mounted from both sides."

"Jeff?" Paula asked, moving to the pony's head. She stroked his nose.

Buck came close to her saying, "Jeff Thompson is my best friend. He's the conservation officer for this area. I may own a ranch, but Jeff knows his horses. He rodeos and trains horses. I don't know a tenth of what he knows."

"But you own a ranch?"

Buck gazed across the wide arena. "Like most ranchers, I taught my horses to do all I needed them to do, but they can learn so much more. If you really want to learn to ride, you should get Jeff to teach you."

Paula nodded and stepped closer. "Well, here goes. Aren't you going to hold his front end for me?"

"No need to. Starfire has been trained to stand still while the rider mounts. He won't move a muscle."

Paula cocked her head sideways and looked the stirrup over. A minute later, she pressed her lips together, twisted them, then asked, "What do I do now?"

"Put your right foot into the stirrup," he said. "Grab onto the horn and pull yourself up. If you can't get your artificial leg over, I'll help you."

She placed her foot into the stirrup, grabbed the horn, and

hoisted herself onto the horse. Her left leg ended up hanging over the horse's rump. Buck gently grabbed hold of the artificial limb and slipped it over. He went around to the pony's left side and pushed Paula's artificial foot into the stirrup.

Paula's face lit up. "This is great! Now what do I do?"

"Release the rein pressure and tell him to walk on."

"Walk on," she said, gingerly holding the reins.

Starfire dutifully carried Paula straight toward the arena fence. "How do I steer?" she called over her shoulder.

"Gently tug on the rein the direction you want to go, and he'll turn."

It didn't take Paula long to catch onto the basics of riding. After fifteen minutes, Buck backed out of the arena and leaned against the fence. He smiled encouragingly for Paula, but he was heartsick inside. Watching the little horse carry Paula reminded him that he missed Sally something awful. He felt a physical pain in his stomach. He loved that little girl as much as he loved her mother. If only there were some way, some hope.

"You okay?" Paula asked, breaking into his thoughts. She had stopped Starfire in front of him.

He looked up at her and blinked. "Sorry," he said. "I was daydreaming."

"I seem to have that affect on you," she said, that teasing expression reappearing.

When he didn't smile back, her eyes searched his. "You're unhappy. I can tell. It's her, isn't it?"

Not wanting to answer, he said, "Show me what you can do. I missed the last few minutes."

More than willing to show off, Paula rode Starfire to the other side of the arena, turned him neatly, and came back. She sure was easy on the eyes. He'd taken her to dinner last night, and they got along quite well. Unfortunately, there were a couple of problems. The biggest one was that Paula didn't know the Lord. She was tolerant of Buck's beliefs but made it clear they weren't for her.

His experience with Alicia in that area had turned out to be a disaster that haunted him to this day. He would let the Lord work in Paula's life in His time. Besides that, he still couldn't forget Alicia. At this point, his feelings were more than stupid; they were insane. Why couldn't he let her go?

When Paula again stopped beside him, he said, "If you're really serious about being a horsewoman, Jeff's your man."

She smiled and slanted her face toward him. "You'll do for now."

When Buck helped her off the horse, she laughed from sheer delight. "That was fabulous! We'll have to do this again soon!" Buck handed her a couple of horse cookies, and she fed them to a willing Starfire. She flashed a broad smile at Buck. "Thank you so much."

"My pleasure," Buck said, grinning down at her.

She glanced at her watch. "I'd better hurry if I'm going to get showered and changed for work this afternoon." She pulled a key ring from the pocket of her jeans. "I noticed you're on Clarence's appointment book."

Buck nodded. "Today we meet with the insurance company's lawyers."

She turned away. "I'll see you then. And thanks again!"

❧

Alicia shifted in her Windsor chair as she sat at Betty Dupre's kitchen table.

Betty asked, "You're really going to go through with this case?"

Uncomfortable, Alicia sipped her tea and nodded.

Betty's expression was kind, almost pitying her. "Do you realize revenge is wrong? And what about forgiveness?"

Alicia stared at the red and blue flower arrangement in the center of the table. Forgiveness had been a common theme in their pastor's recent messages—forgive others as Christ also forgave you.

"It's not about revenge," Alicia murmured finally.

Betty looked surprised. "It's not?"

Alicia said, "It's about justice. Buck caused Garret's death, and he should be held responsible." Those weren't her words. They were Bob Kellerman's. Convicted by the pastor's message last week, she'd brought the very same question to Bob. He'd smiled slightly and set her straight. She wasn't trying to get back at Buck. She was only trying to make sure everyone knew the truth.

Betty set her cup aside and leaned toward Alicia. "I don't believe for one moment that Buck acted out of self-interest when your husband died. You don't think so either, Alicia. You're hurt and confused. I'm afraid you're letting that lawyer push you into doing something you shouldn't. Tell me: Deep down, do you believe the Buck we both know would have let anyone die if he could've prevented it?"

Alicia remembered her time with Buck after the accident. Why couldn't that fairy tale have continued? Why did she have to find out the details of the accident? Buck loved Sally. Maybe they could've been a family. Was it possible that Bob and the police were wrong? Maybe Buck had done the right thing.

If Buck did the right thing, the trial will show it. Bob's words again. Every time they went to dinner, he made sure her thinking was clear, and that she wasn't going to back out.

She glanced at Betty. "I'm not sure," she said. "I don't know anything anymore."

"Don't ruin a good man over this," Betty begged her. "You'll regret it for the rest of your life."

Alicia glanced at the wall clock. "I've got to run, Betty," she said, getting up. "Sally will be home soon, and I have to go meet the bus." She started for the door, but Betty's hand on her arm made her pause.

"Think very carefully about this. Pray about it. Never do anything you don't have peace with God about."

Alicia flashed the older woman a tight smile. "Okay."

She grabbed her coat and left Betty Dupre's home. The sky was overcast, and a mistlike rain cooled her face. She looked upward and whispered a prayer for guidance. Should she turn the other cheek even in this horrible situation?

She suddenly wished she'd had God in her life years earlier, back when Buck had first found Him. Then none of this would have happened. Her life would have taken a completely different road.

Guilt speared her. What was she thinking? Garret hadn't been a perfect husband, but he'd given her Sally. It was wrong for her to wish for anything different.

Beside the highway, Alicia stood and watched the traffic whiz by. It wasn't long before the big yellow bus stopped, its lights flashing. Sally bounded down the steps and skipped toward her. Watching Sally, Alicia knew without a doubt that Sally was all that mattered. With careful budgeting, she could probably stretch the insurance money another four months. If she lost the court case, her little girl would become a latchkey kid. What could be worse than that?

❧

Buck pushed open the door to Clarence Brown's office in Prince George. Paula sat behind her desk, an earphone in her ear, typing away. Her hair was pinned up. She wore a gray business suit with a white blouse and had on light makeup.

She looked up and gave him a brilliant smile. "Hey, long time no see."

Buck grinned. "Yeah. It's gotta be at least three hours."

She laughed. "Thanks so much for letting me ride Starfire. I really enjoyed myself."

"We'll do it again soon, but I think I'm going to call Jeff in to instruct you. You've got the gift, and you need a real teacher."

"The gift?"

Buck nodded. "When folks are real serious about horses, they can't keep their hands off of them. That's you. You're a natural."

She grew thoughtful. "You're making my dreams come true, Buck. There's no way I can thank you enough." With another, softer smile, she pressed an intercom button and announced that Buck had arrived.

Clarence's door opened, and he stepped into the waiting room. His thin face looked grim. "Come on in."

When Buck entered the office, two men were already seated in front of Clarence's desk. Clarence pulled up a chair from the back wall and stationed it so Buck could face the two men.

"Buck," Clarence began when they were seated, "these gentlemen represent the insurance company. This is Ron Parker."

A heavyset man with thick eyebrows and a droopy chin, Parker nodded. "How do you do, Connelly?" He was dressed in a rumpled brown suit.

"Fine," Buck said, to be polite. Judging from Clarence's face, Buck wasn't sure he should be fine.

Clarence continued with the introductions. "And this is Martin Del."

Del was closest to Buck and offered his hand. His grip was weak, his palms cool. The lawyer was thin, his jet black hair slicked back, and his suit must have cost more than a prize bull.

Clarence leaned back in his chair. "Well, gentlemen, why don't you explain your position on this matter?"

Del crossed his ankle over his knee. "It's like this, Mr. Connelly. We're sure that this lawsuit is not covered under the fire hall's policy."

Buck leaned forward in his seat. "Come again?"

"We've reviewed the file," Martin Del said, "and it's our opinion that you were not in the performance of your normal fire-fighting duties when Garret Simmons died."

Buck looked at Clarence. "What are they talking about?"

Clarence motioned toward Del. "I'd rather he explained it."

Buck locked eyes with Del. "It was a car accident. The car caught fire. We put the fire out. That's what firefighters do."

Del stretched his lips into the semblance of a smile. "Your partner wanted to effect a rescue, and you physically prevented him. It's our understanding that you've had a long-time fascination with the deceased man's wife, and at one point the RCMP were considering charging you with murder. We maintain that you were working out of self-interest that day. Because of it, a man died. We don't see why we should pay."

Buck's head snapped back toward Clarence. "Tell me this isn't true."

Clarence drummed his fingers on his desk. "It shouldn't be true."

Del picked up a leather brief case. "I think we've discussed everything." He and his partner stood.

Buck jumped to his feet to block Martin Del's way. "When I joined the department, I was told we had insurance, that we were protected. Wait until the other members find out they're not insured."

Del smirked. "They're insured for the normal duties of a firefighter. Normal duties don't include killing the husband of the woman you're obsessed with."

Buck's hand bunched into a fist. He started to raise it when Clarence's voice roped him in. "Let it go, Buck. This is far from over."

Del sidestepped Buck, his partner following. "Thank you for your time," he said to Clarence, then paused at the door and looked toward Buck. "Mr. Connelly, you'll be getting a letter from the chief of your fire hall. We've informed him that we will not cover you for any future fire-fighting duties."

Buck felt like he'd been thrown from a horse. "You mean I'm out of the fire department too?"

Del stared at him a moment before saying, "That's exactly what I mean." The two lawyers left the office.

Buck collapsed into his chair, the air rushing from his lungs. He looked at Clarence like a drowning man looking at a life preserver.

Clarence took the seat next to him. "When there is an insurance claim, the first rule is to find a reason not to pay. That's what these guys are doing. They've found a reason not to pay."

"Are they right?" Buck asked. "Did I act outside of the normal duties of a firefighter?"

Clarence shook his head. "Not a chance. Preventing another firefighter from doing something stupid is a normal duty. If it had been anyone other than Garret Simmons in that car, there wouldn't even be a question. They'd be paying."

Buck rubbed his face with both hands. Clarence waited without speaking. Finally, Buck asked, "Where do we go from here?"

"We could sue the insurance company, but. . ."

"But what?" Buck asked. He wanted to sue someone real bad. The insurance company seemed like a good place to start.

"Fifty thousand would be the minimum cost to sue those

guys. That figure could easily run up to a couple hundred thousand, and they know it. It's what they're banking on. To be honest, your relationship with Alicia Simmons clouds the issue. Given the right judge or jury, we could spend all that money and still lose."

Buck held his hands out in a pleading gesture. "What do I do?"

"Offer to settle," the lawyer said. "We offer to pay Alicia Simmons whatever you can afford. It's a protective move. Folks already have opinions regarding your guilt or innocence. I'll phrase the offer so there is no admission on your part. Considering there's no insurance involved, they'll take it. Kellerman was counting on a fat juicy insurance check. He's not going to waste time and money in court if he knows the money amount won't change. What's the most you can raise?"

Drawing in a breath, Buck leaned back in the chair, leaned his head back, and closed his eyes. "I could sell off most of the herd. It's the wrong time of year, so I'd probably only get a hundred thousand dollars after income tax. I can mortgage the ranch for three hundred thousand." He looked at Clarence, despair in his eyes. "I can come up with four hundred thousand dollars."

"If you sell off your herd, how will you make a living?"

He looked down at his callused hands. "I'll get a job."

Clarence Brown pursed his lips and returned to his seat to make a note on his legal pad. "Four hundred thousand is a pretty good chunk of change. We'll offer Kellerman three hundred thousand and see if you can keep the herd."

"Think he'll go for it?"

"Absolutely. No lawyer in his right mind would turn down an offer like that."

thirteen

In spite of Clarence's expectations, Alicia did turn down Buck's offer to settle out of court. A year later, Buck sat with Clarence in a courthouse conference room in Prince George. Eyes bloodshot and his face haggard from lack of sleep, Buck took a sip of strong coffee and set the Styrofoam cup on the long oak table. Clarence Brown sat across from him, turning pages in a folder.

Buck leaned forward. "I still can't believe we're doing this."

"Neither can I," Clarence said, shuffling papers. "They should have taken your settlement. According to Kellerman, Alicia Simmons wants to hear a judge say you killed her husband."

Buck rubbed his eyes. "Clarence, that doesn't sound like the new her."

Clarence looked up from the file. "The new her?"

Buck looked down at his clenched hands.

"You're not keeping something from me, are you, Buck?"

Buck looked up. "Her best friend is the wife of the fire department chief. I heard through the grapevine that Alicia has become a Christian—that she's changed."

Brown flipped through some more papers. Without looking up he said, "Thanks for filling me in on Alicia Simmons's statement of faith, but it won't help us here."

Buck drained his cup in one quick motion. "Look, why don't we plead guilty and get it over with? You already said I'll probably lose."

"That's right," Clarence said, squinting at Buck. "I said

you'd *probably* lose. You just might win."

"What if I don't want to win?" Buck pulled a small chip from the edge of his cup and dropped it inside.

Clarence stared at him, brow lowered. "Why wouldn't you want to win?"

Buck kept his head down. "I heard that Alicia's insurance money is gone. Things are getting pretty tight for her." He looked up at Clarence. "Sally has to go to after-school day care because Alicia has an evening job. Truth is, if it weren't for this lawsuit, I'd want to help her out, anyway. Why don't I plead guilty and give her the money?"

Clarence's folder snapped shut. He leaned forward. "If you plead guilty, the RCMP will charge you with murder. The only reason they haven't up until now is their circumstantial evidence doesn't support a conviction. If you get up in court and say, 'Yeah, I was responsible for Garret Simmons's death,' you won't get out of this building without handcuffs on."

Buck felt like he'd been doused with cold water. His chest tightened until he could hardly breathe. "Okay," he said, reluctantly, "I guess we fight."

&

Alicia Simmons rubbed her weary eyes. She'd slept a full hour the night before. This whole thing was wrong. She knew it without a doubt. Her talks with Betty, the sermons at church, and even her own Bible reading told her that suing Buck was wrong. Brother shouldn't go against brother in court. Why didn't she just call it off?

She pressed cold fingers against her temples and knew she couldn't stop these legal wheels from turning. She had to think of Sally.

Betty Dupre was able to watch Sally two evenings a week, but on the other three days, Alicia had to drop her daughter off at a day care. Alicia knew several other parents who did the same thing, but she still felt that she was betraying Sally. Her little girl wasn't over her father's death or the shock of Buck's involvement. Now the poor kid had to be dumped off at a stranger's house three nights a week. She didn't get into her own bed until past eleven o'clock. The Bible also said that she had to look after her daughter, didn't it?

"It still bugs me that they never offered to settle." Alicia told Bob Kellerman, who sat near her at the dark oak table in the conference room at the courthouse.

Kellerman looked up from his file. "I'm sorry, Dear. What did you say?"

"I said, it bugs me they never offered to settle. Why are they going through with this? You said they're bound to loose."

Kellerman lifted one shoulder and let it drop. "It baffles me too. Clarence Brown said that Buck didn't want his good name tarnished." He smiled at her as though talking to a child. "It doesn't say much for a man when he thinks more about his good name than those he's hurt, does it?"

Alicia's nervous fingers wound around a curl near her ear. "That doesn't sound like Buck. I can see him hating me, but not Sally."

Kellerman leaned across the table and took her hand. "Have you ever gone hunting?"

Alicia shook her head. "No. Why?"

"Well, I have. Do you know what tortures a hunter more than anything else?"

Alicia waited for him to go on.

"The animal that got away. You had the beautiful elk in your sights, you're just about to squeeze the trigger, and someone steps on a branch. *Poof*, it's gone. That elk haunts you in your dreams. It was almost yours. Its head was going to hang on your wall as a testimony to your skill, but now it's just a fleeting memory. It gnaws at you, and you never rest.

Deep inside, there's a hope that you'll see it again and get to finish the job."

Alicia tucked the curl behind her ear. "Are you saying I'm an elk?"

Kellerman squeezed her hand. "Far from it. You're a beautiful woman, but to Buck you might just be an elk. He lost you after high school and couldn't rest until he captured you again. The fact you got away a second time is probably driving him crazy."

Not wanting to meet Kellerman's probing gaze, Alicia stared at the wood grain on the table. She slipped her hand from his. She wasn't just a trophy to Buck. When he played with Sally, he was open, honest, and true. Not a whiff of pretense there. Whatever Buck's reasons were for going through with this case, they had nothing to do with big game hunting.

A phone on the table rang. Kellerman picked it up. "Yes," he said into the receiver. "Good, we'll be right there."

He stood and held out his hand to her. "It's show time."

Alicia ignored his hand and got up from the table. Always the gentleman, Kellerman opened the door for her, and she stepped out into the spacious courthouse lobby. A dozen couches sat in corners, in central groupings, and along the walls for witnesses awaiting their turns to testify. Two stories above them was a copper dome ceiling, the building's crowning glory.

The courtroom wasn't at all what Alicia had expected. Having grown up with Perry Mason television programs, Alicia expected a room the size of an auditorium and jammed with spectators. Here the judge sat behind a desk on an elevated platform. A spectator area contained half a dozen rows of seats. At the fore stood two tables, one for each party to the suit. To the left was a witness stand with a chair behind a wooden railing, and in the center, a platinum-haired court reporter sat at a small table.

At the table to the right, Buck sat with his lawyer. Next to him was the red-haired young woman she'd seen with Buck in the restaurant.

She followed Bob Kellerman to the left table. When he pulled out her seat, she sat down and glanced up to catch Buck watching her. His head hung low between slumped shoulders. She saw something in his eyes. . .*regret?* The woman put her hand on Buck's arm and squeezed.

"I thought spectators had to sit back there," Alicia said to Kellerman and pointed to the seats behind them where half a dozen people sat.

Her lawyer shot a quick look at the defense table. "She's not a spectator. She's Brown's legal secretary. I think she's his niece as well."

A door opened, and the judge walked in.

The clerk stood and called out, "All rise for his Honor, Rawinder Singh."

The judge was an East Indian man in his late fifties. Dressed in a red robe with white trim, he appeared quite fit. He sat down, surveyed the courtroom, and smiled. "Please sit down." His voice sounded pleasant.

While everyone found their seats, the judge perused a file before him. He looked first at Buck, then at Alicia. "We are here today to decide the matter between Alicia Simmons and Buck Connelly, a suit for wrongful death asking for damages of two million dollars. Is this correct?"

Kellerman stood and said, "Yes, Your Honor."

Buck's lawyer did likewise.

"Let's proceed," the judge said. "Mr. Kellerman, your opening remarks."

A door behind them opened, and Alicia glanced back to see Sergeant Meyers take a seat. Kellerman had mentioned that Meyers would be at the trial, hoping to find enough evidence to press criminal charges. Several months ago, Alicia would have been glad to hear it. Now, she prayed it wouldn't happen. The thought that Buck had really meant to kill her husband. . . She blinked back sudden, unexpected tears.

Kellerman stood. As the defendant, Buck could choose trial by judge or jury. He'd selected judge only.

Kellerman buttoned his sleek, Italian coat and stepped forward. "Your Honor, this is a simple case, and I won't waste the court's time with a long address. We will present witnesses to show that Buck Connelly—whether with or without malice—was the direct cause of the death of Garret Simmons. We believe we can prove on the balance of probabilities that Mr. Connelly," he pointed at Buck, "prevented the rescue of Garret Simmons which resulted in Mr. Simmons's death by fire. Thank you." He sat down.

Alicia bit down on her lip, forcing back insistent tears. Garret had died a horrible death. *Please, Lord, don't let it be true that Buck did this.*

Kellerman's hand was over hers. "Go ahead and cry. It'll help us with the judge."

The tears suddenly dried up. She turned sharply toward Bob Kellerman. She'd finally had enough. "That's it. I want to drop this."

Kellerman squeezed her hand until it hurt. "You can't drop it," he whispered. "The plane is in the air. No one gets off."

Alicia turned to the judge and tried to stand, but Kellerman gripped her jacket under the table and held her down. He leaned over and whispered in her ear. "If you stop this trial, I'll sue you. If you bothered to read our contract, my fee is contingent upon you winning unless you stop the suit. You're obligated to pay my fees. On a two-million-dollar lawsuit, we're talking eight hundred thousand dollars. If you think

Sally being in day care is bad, wait until I take your house. Now sit down and keep your mouth shut."

Alicia went cold. Horrified, she stared at the man beside her. He was a monster, a sweetly smiling, flattering crook. What had she gotten herself into? Her mouth came open as she gasped for air. The room seemed to close in on her. Pressing her arms close to her body, she shifted away from Kellerman and tried to breathe. *God, help me!*

"Your Honor," Buck's lawyer began. "The defense will show that Mr. Connelly acted properly in his duties as a firefighter, and that Mr. Simmons's accident, while tragic, was just that, an accident. No one was to blame. No one was at fault. Thank you."

The judge scribbled some notes, then turned toward Kellerman. "Call your first witness."

Kellerman stood. "I call Jeff Thompson to the stand."

The court reporter spoke into a microphone. Seconds later, Jeff Thompson entered the courtroom wearing his conservation officer's uniform. He stood before the witness stand. The court reporter swore him in, and Jeff took a seat behind the rail.

Kellerman approached the witness stand. "Mr. Thompson, thank you for coming today."

"It's not like I had any choice." Thompson glanced at Buck, apology in his eyes. Would he tell the truth? Somehow Alicia hoped he wouldn't. If they lost the case, Kellerman wouldn't get paid, and they could get on with their lives.

"I understand," Kellerman said. "Are you and Mr. Connelly good friends?"

"Best friends," Thompson said.

Kellerman turned to Judge Singh. "In light of the close friendship between Mr. Thompson and Mr. Connelly, I'd like to treat Mr. Thompson as a hostile witness."

Judge Singh scratched his ear. "Why don't we wait for Mr. Thompson to show some hostility? As a conservation officer, Mr. Thompson is a peace officer and an officer of this court. Unless he gives us reason to believe otherwise, we'll presume that Mr. Thompson will answer all questions fully and truthfully."

Kellerman gave a tight nod. "Yes, Your Honor."

Alicia drew in a long breath and relaxed a little. She stole a quick look at Buck. He stared straight ahead, expressionless.

"Mr. Thompson," Kellerman continued, "were you present at the accident scene where Garret Simmons died?"

"Yes."

Kellerman walked to Alicia and sat down beside her. "Good. Then, keeping in mind, as Judge Singh said, that you are an officer of this court and sworn to tell the truth, please tell us all the relevant details that happened at the accident scene."

Jeff Thompson looked uncertain. Buck's lawyer whispered in Buck's ear. He didn't seem pleased. Slowly, carefully, Jeff Thompson recited the details surrounding Garret's death. Alicia knew the entire story by now, but she still hurt to hear Jeff Thompson describe how Buck stopped him from rescuing Garret. "That's it," Jeff said.

Kellerman rose and walked to the witness stand. "Let me get this right. You were prepared to go down the embankment and pull Garret Simmons from the car in spite of the power line?"

"Yes," Jeff said.

"You weren't afraid the line was live, that you might've been injured?"

Jeff Thompson averted his eyes. "Not at the time. Since then. . ."

"I don't want to hear about since then," Kellerman interrupted. "Why were you unafraid the day of the accident?"

"The transformer was all smashed, and the breaker switch had blown."

"So, if Mr. Connelly had not physically stopped you, you would've rescued Garret Simmons?"

"Yes," Jeff said.

"Thank you," Bob Kellerman said and sat down. "This is going to be easier than I thought," he whispered to Alicia.

She stiffened and refused to look at him.

Clarence Brown stood and walked to the witness stand. "Mr. Thompson, you said 'not at the time.' What did you mean by that?"

Jeff Thompson leaned forward, a smile on his face. "Since the accident. . ."

Kellerman shot to his feet. "Objection, Your Honor. We are here to deal with the facts of that day. If Mr. Brown wants to bring something into evidence, it should be factual and relevant."

"Sustained."

Clarence Brown returned to his table and glanced at his notes. He asked Jeff Thompson a few more questions, but nothing Jeff Thompson said could undo the damage of his testimony. Finally, he left the stand.

Judge Singh glanced at his watch. "If no one has any objections, let's break for an early lunch and come back at one o'clock." He didn't wait for anyone to object. The judge stood, everyone rose, and he left the courtroom.

fourteen

Half an hour later, in a corner booth in Maggie's Family Restaurant, Buck cut a tiny piece from his rib eye steak. The meat was nicely seasoned and tender, but his stomach wasn't in the mood for food right now. Across from him, Paula dug into her lasagna, and Clarence attacked his sirloin. There was a strange grin on Paula's face each time she looked at Buck.

"Hey, don't be so glum," Clarence said, sipping cola. "We knew Jeff's testimony would be damaging. He's only the first witness. We'll bounce back."

"Right," Buck said, not believing it.

"I think the judge likes you," Paula added. "He sure was quick to put Kellerman in his place."

"Eat up," Clarence said, looking at Buck's untouched fries. "It's going to be a long day."

Buck cut a sliver of juicy beef and popped it into his mouth. It might as well be cardboard. "Do we have to present a defense?"

Clarence choked, reached for his glass, and drank. "Of course we have to," he said, looking at Buck as though he doubted his sanity.

Buck laid down his fork. "It would be so much easier if we let Kellerman do his thing, then go home."

"Not a chance," Clarence replied. "If we don't present a defense, you could sue me."

"I wouldn't sue you," Buck said, disgusted by the idea.

Clarence looked him full in the face. "Right now, you're confused and hurt. You don't know what you want. Once the sheriff shows up and throws you out of your home, you'll be looking for someone to blame, and that person would be me." His expression grew grim. "If you don't want to present a defense, I resign. Effective immediately." He stared at Buck until Paula broke the tension by touching Buck's arm.

"This is about Alicia, isn't it?" she asked gently.

He nodded and looked down.

She said, "I can see how she'd be hard to forget."

"It's not just her." Buck turned to stare at the closed window blind beside him.

"There's someone else?" Paula asked.

"There's Sally. It tears me apart when I think of what she's been through." He swallowed. "I want to help both of them."

Paula sipped coffee. "Losing the case isn't the way to help them," she said, returning her cup to its saucer.

Buck turned to her. "It isn't?"

"It isn't," Clarence said, iron in his voice.

A soft smile lit up Paula's face. "Winning the case is the way to help her."

"That doesn't make sense. Alicia needs money. She has to win."

"Listen," Paula said, leaning in. "If she wins, Bob Kellerman gets almost half of the settlement."

Buck looked shocked. "Half?"

"Pretty much," Clarence told him. "He's doing this case on contingency. He gets a percentage of what she wins. Depending on how the agreement is written up, he could get close to half."

"If you win," Paula added, "you could secretly donate the money she needs through a church or something, and Kellerman would get nothing."

Buck looked at Clarence. "Is that right?"

Clarence wiped steak sauce from his mouth with a napkin.

"Paula's hit the bull's eye." He beamed at her, then said to Buck, "It's embarrassing. I've been trying to think of a way to motivate you, and here my niece comes up with the answer."

She playfully punched Clarence's shoulder. "Hey, I was a cop before I became a secretary. I'm not just a pretty face, you know." She looked directly at Buck. "And I know something about 100 Mile House you haven't told us."

Buck shifted in his chair. *That was confidential. How could she know?*

"What?" Clarence said.

"Buck hasn't been totally forthcoming about the events after 100 Mile House. My buddies at the detachment down there say Buck has been back several times to see someone."

"Who?" Clarence said.

"Someone who could win us this case," Paula said, smiling. "We just need Buck to sign one little form, and we win."

Clarence locked eyes with Buck. "Okay, Connelly, spill."

Buck looked from Clarence, to Paula, then back again. It was hard for a man to admit weakness, but if there were ever two people he could trust, it was them. Buck told them why he went back to 100 Mile House and who he saw.

Clarence Brown's jaw was tight. "I should knock you senseless. Why did you keep this from me?"

Buck toyed with his food, then looked up at Clarence. "At first, I didn't say anything because I was embarrassed. Later, when I realized it would help me win, I kept my mouth shut, because up until now, I didn't want to win."

Clarence grinned. "Well, once we get that guy up here, this game is about to change." He looked over at Paula. "And why didn't you say anything?"

"I just found out this morning. Besides, I felt it was Buck's decision, not mine."

A deep voice brought them all around. "Can a witness eat

with the defendant? That is, if the defendant is still my friend."
Jeff Thompson stood beside Buck. He was fidgeting with his
uniform cap.

"Absolutely." Buck slid over, and Jeff took the seat beside him.

"Jeff, meet my defense team: Clarence Brown and his
niece, Paula."

Jeff shook hands with each of them. His hand lingered
longer in Paula's, and his gaze held hers a little longer, as
well. Paula's smile deepened.

"I should caution you that we cannot discuss the trial,"
Clarence told Jeff.

"That's okay," Buck said. "We can talk about horses. Paula
is learning how to ride."

Jeff looked at Paula and smiled. "No kidding."

"It's a childhood dream of mine. I never had time to learn
until now. Buck's been giving me lessons."

"That's great," Jeff said.

The slim waiter appeared, and Jeff ordered a duplicate of
Buck's lunch. When they were alone again, Buck said, "I've
taken her as far as I can, Jeff. She's a natural."

Jeff turned his attention to Paula. "What has he taught you?"

Paula's brown eyes sparkled. "I can do a walk, trot, lope,
and a couple of times, I've galloped. But because of my. . ."
She paused, and her cheeks flamed.

"What?" Jeff said, glancing at Buck for help.

"She has an artificial leg," Buck said.

Paula's eyes flashed toward him. She looked like she
wanted to bolt from the table.

Jeff's expression didn't change. "Above or below the knee?"

"Above," Paula said. She relaxed a little as Jeff went on.

"Buck's right," he said, "You've gone as far as you can
with him teaching you. When dealing with an artificial limb,

you have to use different methods to give the horse the cues it needs for the more intricate maneuvers."

"Hey, I've done pretty good so far," Buck said.

"For a rancher," Jeff replied, sending him a wry grin. He turned back to Paula. "Mind you, if all you want to do is trail riding, then Buck has taught you all you need to know."

Paula shook her head. "No way. I want to learn it all. When I was a little girl, I used to spend hours in the backyard riding a broomstick horse. I actually joined the RCMP hoping to get into the musical ride, but they found other uses for me instead. If there's more, I want to learn it." They spoke at length about riding and dealing with her handicap. Jeff seemed to put Paula at ease.

Jeff lifted his arm from the table so the waiter could set down his lunch, then he continued, "I work with a group out at a local stable. You'd be more than welcome to join us."

Paula clenched her fist and punched the air. "All right!" Looking behind Buck, her smiled faded. "Oh no," she whispered.

Buck turned to see what had caught her attention. Suddenly, his heart lurched.

Ten paces away, Alicia was striding toward their table, her gaze on him. She stepped close to him and stammered, "Buck, I. . ."

"Wait a minute, Mrs. Simmons," Clarence said, holding up a hand as though stopping traffic. "It is improper for you to talk with my client during the trial. Your lawyer should have told you that."

Alicia stood, gulping short breaths. Her hands were clenched on her purse strap.

Buck's throat tightened until he thought he'd suffocate. He wanted to jump to his feet, take her in his arms, and tell her that everything would be all right. His love for Alicia was a physical pain.

"Buck," she said, finally, "I just want to say, no matter what happens. . .I forgive you, and I hope someday you'll forgive me." She looked into his eyes, and the world stood still.

Had he heard her right? Instead of anger, her eyes showed brokenness. And regret.

She took a deep breath. "There's something else you need to know. Kellerman. . ."

Out of nowhere, Bob Kellerman appeared at her side. He gripped her elbow, and she winced. "My apologies," Kellerman said, his perfect smile in place. "My client is a little emotional right now. Come along, Alicia."

She didn't resist as he guided her away, but once, she glanced back at Buck, a pleading look on her face.

"That was weird," Paula said, staring after them.

"No kidding," Jeff said.

"I don't like that guy," Paula said. "If I were still a cop, I'd examine his laundry under a microscope. I'd say he's controlling her. That poor girl looks like she needs help."

"Let's help her by beating Kellerman." Buck pushed his half-finished plate away. His fists clenched, the muscles in his arms knotted. If Kellerman hurt her, the next time he'd be on trial, it would be because he was guilty.

❧

"You're hurting me," Alicia told Bob Kellerman as he forced her out of the restaurant.

"Whose fault is that?" he demanded. The pressure on her arm stayed the same. Outside, he walked her around the building until they were hidden from view and pushed her against the clay brick wall of the restaurant. He leaned over her, his hand against her chin, pushing her back into the rough bricks. "What do you think you were doing in there?"

Her eyes filled with tears. "I wanted to tell him I forgave him. Is that so awful?"

Kellerman bunched his other hand into a fist, and Alicia shrank away.

"You still don't get it, do you?"

"You're hurting me." She drew in a breath to scream, but Kellerman clamped her mouth closed. His hot breath puffed against her face as he said, "If you mess up this case for me, it's going to cost you. This is a bad world, Alicia, with bad people in it. A woman with a little girl isn't safe. Especially the little girl." He suddenly turned her loose and stepped back.

Alicia's knees buckled. She scraped her hand on the brick, trying to keep from falling. "What do you want from me?"

His blue gaze piercing her, he straightened his coat and adjusted his cuffs. "I want you to shut up and let me win this case." He turned away and strode into the parking lot.

Alicia slid to her knees and sobbed.

❧

When they were all seated in the courthouse that afternoon, Buck looked over at Alicia. Her cheeks had dark streaks on them like her mascara had run, and she couldn't repair the damage. She looked back at Buck and sent him a pitiful smile. *What's going on?* Buck steeled himself and looked up at the judge.

"Mr. Kellerman, are you ready to begin?"

Kellerman stood. "Yes, Your Honor. I call Karen Russell to the stand."

Seconds later, Karen Russell entered the courtroom and was sworn in. She wore a dark skirt and a light blue blouse. Her hair hung loose about her shoulders.

"Ms. Russell," Kellerman began questioning, "do you know the defendant?"

"Yes," she said, looking at Buck.

"How well?"

"We were engaged once."

"For how long?" Kellerman asked.

Karen Russell dabbed at her eyes with a tissue. "Almost two years."

"Why didn't you marry?"

Karen's eyes narrowed, and she looked over at Alicia. "He told me he was still in love with Alicia Simmons."

Kellerman paused and rubbed his forehead. "Correct me if I'm wrong, but wasn't Alicia Simmons married at the time?"

"Yes," Karen said, "but that didn't seem to matter to Buck."

"Did you mention to him that he was in love with a married woman?"

Karen bit down on her lip and hesitated. "Yes, I did. He seemed to think there was still hope."

Buck grabbed Clarence's arm. "I never said that," he whispered into his lawyer's ear. "I said I couldn't get her out of my mind, and it would be wrong to marry Karen."

Clarence nodded but said nothing.

As Kellerman continued the questioning, Karen's replies were often vague and always damaging to Buck. Glancing at Alicia, Buck noticed that Alicia seemed as distressed as he was at the direction the case was going.

Clarence Brown cross-examined Karen, but she seemed to have an answer for everything. When he released the witness and sat down, he shook his head in disgust.

Next, Kellerman called Craig Denman, one of Buck's friends from church. Craig was a tall, spindly man who wore thick glasses.

"Mr. Denman," Kellerman said, "how long have you known the defendant?"

"About twelve years," Denman said.

"Did you know him after he broke up with Alicia Simmons?"

"Yes," Denman answered.

"What was Mr. Connelly's mental state at that time?"

Clarence Brown jumped to his feet. "Objection. The witness is not an expert."

"Overruled," Judge Singh said. "This is a civil trial. I'd like to hear what Mr. Denman has to say."

"He was devastated for the first couple of weeks," Denman said, peering at Kellerman.

"But he got over it, didn't he?" Kellerman asked, smiling.

Buck shrank into his seat. He realized where this was heading, and it wasn't going to be pretty.

Denman shifted uncomfortably in his seat.

"You go to the same church as the defendant, don't you?" Kellerman asked.

"Yes, Sir," Denman said, glancing at Buck.

"Well, you just swore on a Bible, so I expect the truth."

Denman sent a look of apology toward Buck. "After Bible study one evening, Buck suddenly brightened up. He'd been depressed for weeks."

"More detail, please, Mr. Denman."

"We were studying about how God always turns a bad situation to good. Buck seemed to latch onto that."

"What did he say, Mr. Denman?"

"He told me that somehow, someway, he'd get Alicia back. That God would make sure of it."

Judge Singh's eyebrows nearly reached his hairline. He shifted in his seat and looked closer at the witness.

Kellerman spent the afternoon with a parade of witnesses who testified that Buck had told them he still loved Alicia, how he'd never married because he couldn't forget her. Buck hadn't realized how many people he'd shared his feelings with.

Kellerman saved the best for last when he called Sergeant Larry Meyers to the stand. Dressed in his RCMP uniform, Meyers was sworn in and looked quite relaxed in the witness seat.

"Sergeant Meyers," Kellerman said, "was Garret Simmons's death an accident?"

Clarence again shot to his feet. "Objection! This trial is about whether or not Buck Connelly acted properly when he prevented Jeff Thompson from affecting a rescue. Sergeant Meyers wasn't there, and any information on a criminal investigation is not relevant."

Judge Singh tapped his desk with a pencil. "I want to hear what Sergeant Meyers has to say."

"But, Your Honor," Clarence said, "this is a civil suit. If the police investigation were relevant, criminal charges would have been filed."

Judge Singh took a sip of water. "Mr. Brown, you elected to have trial by judge. If there were a jury present, I might be more inclined to agree with you. However, since it is I who decides wrongdoing here, I want to hear everything. If in my deliberations I decide I shouldn't have allowed certain testimony, I will not use it in my decision."

Clarence sank into his seat, his jaw set.

"You may continue," the judge told Bob Kellerman.

"Sergeant Meyers," Kellerman said, "was Garret Simmons's death an accident?"

Sergeant Meyers leaned forward in his chair. "Based on my investigation, I would rule his death a homicide."

Kellerman leaned against his table. "What led you to that conclusion?"

"The brake line had been tampered with."

"Did you have any suspects?"

Clarence Brown started to rise, but one look from the judge sent him back to his seat.

"Yes," Sergeant Meyers said. "We only found one man with means, motive, and opportunity."

"And who was that?"

Meyers looked straight at Buck. "The defendant, Buck Connelly."

"You said something about a motive. What was that?"

Meyers turned toward the judge. "We considered Buck Connelly's obsession with Alicia Simmons to be a motive."

"And means?" Kellerman continued.

"I visited Buck Connelly's home and found a shop full of mechanic's tools. I also learned from Mr. Connelly's farmhand that the defendant is skilled in auto mechanics."

"Why wasn't he charged at that time?"

Meyers shrugged. "He would have been, if it were up to me. Crown Counsel felt the evidence was too circumstantial for a conviction. There was too much room for reasonable doubt."

"What about a balance of probabilities?" Kellerman asked.

Clarence Brown was on his feet. "Please, Your Honor, calls for a verdict on behalf of the witness. I object."

"I agree," Judge Singh said. "The witness will not answer that question."

"I have no more questions," Kellerman said, rounding the table to take his seat.

Clarence Brown approached Sergeant Meyers. "Tell me, Sergeant, who decided that the brakes were tampered with?"

"I did," the sergeant answered.

"And are you a forensics expert?" Brown asked.

"No, but I have years of experience."

"But you're not an expert? You have no formal mechanical training?"

"No."

"Tell me," Brown said. "These people who told you Buck was obsessed with Mrs. Simmons—did you ever dig deeper to find out if they had a motive to speak ill of Mr. Connelly? Did you consider that Karen Russell's statement might be nothing more than the revenge of a bitter, jilted woman?"

"I had no reason to," Meyers replied, looking the lawyer in the eye.

"Sergeant Meyers, is it possible that the reason Crown Counsel chose not to file charges was because they didn't have any case at all?"

Sergeant Meyers started to open his mouth.

"Don't bother answering," Clarence Brown said. "I think the facts speaks for themselves. I'm finished, your Honor."

Judge Singh turned his attention to Bob Kellerman. "Any more witnesses?"

"No, Your Honor."

"Then we stand in recess until tomorrow." Everyone rose as the judge left, then sat down again.

Clarence turned to Buck. "Don't be too discouraged. We knew their case would be built on your feelings for Alicia. Tomorrow, it's our turn. We've got some pretty good ammunition, not to mention a secret weapon you didn't tell me about."

Buck looked over at Alicia. She had her head bent down so he couldn't see her face. "For Alicia's sake," Buck said, "I hope so."

fifteen

The next morning, Alicia slipped into the ladies' room at the courthouse to double check her makeup. She peered into the mirror at a woman twice her age with sunken, dark eyes and lines about her mouth. She had tossed and turned until close to four A.M., then crawled out of bed at six-thirty to face a barrage of questions from a concerned Sally. Trying to think of evasive answers that would satisfy Sally was more exhausting than punching her pillow all night. Alicia was in deep trouble, and she had no one to turn to.

Bob Kellerman met her outside the courtroom.

"Good morning," he said, bursting with good cheer. "You look wonderful." When she sent him a disbelieving look, he said, "The more stressed out you look, the more sympathetic Judge Singh will be. We have to use every bit of ammunition we can, my dear."

Once he said that, Alicia wanted to run home to redo her hair and makeup and try and look as though she hadn't a care in the world. Unfortunately, there was no way she could keep the turmoil in her heart from showing on her face.

When they entered the courtroom, she didn't dare look over at Buck's table. Last night, she'd settled in her own mind that Buck wasn't responsible for Garret's death. Yesterday's testimony had proven that Buck truly loved her. He would have never hurt Garret, because doing so would have hurt her.

Oh, to turn back the clock! Instead of sending Buck away in the rain that night, she should have let him in and heard him out. All she'd ever truly wanted had been within her grasp, and she'd let it slip away. Buck would never want her now—not after what she'd done to him.

"Please rise," the court clerk said.

Alicia stood with everyone else. Judge Singh took his seat, and they all sat down. "Please begin," he said to Clarence Brown.

Buttoning his gray suit coat, Clarence Brown got to his feet. "I'd like to call Roger Portman to the stand."

A tall, muscular man entered the courtroom. Though he was only in his midthirties, his head was shaved bald. He wore brown slacks and a white cotton dress shirt open at the neck. The court reporter swore him in.

"What is your occupation?" Clarence asked.

"I work for the BC Hydro and Power Authority. I'm a lineman."

"And what does a lineman do?" Brown asked.

Portman kept rubbing his hands together in a nervous gesture. "I'm responsible for installing, connecting, and disconnecting power lines and related equipment. Basically, if it carries power, and it belongs to the company, I work with it."

"How long have you been doing this?"

"Ten years and five months," Portman answered.

"Tell me, if a power line is lying on the ground, and the switch has blown, is it necessarily dead?"

Portman shook his head. "Absolutely not. Power lines that run along the highway are high voltage. If one line is knocked down, it can draw current from the lines above and transmit it to the ground. That's called induction."

Clarence put a hand on his hip. "What's the best thing to do when encountering downed power lines?"

Portman grew confident. "Stay away from them and call us. If you're trapped in a car, stay in the car."

"Thank you. No further questions." Clarence Brown said.

He smiled at the judge and returned to his table. "Your witness," the judge told Kellerman.

Kellerman stood and approached the witness. "Mr. Portman, am I correct that you were the lineman who responded to the Simmons's accident?"

"Yes, Sir."

"Was the power line live? Was it carrying current from induction?"

"No," Portman said. "When the transformer blew, it blew the breakers on the lines above."

"Mr. Thompson testified that he'd noted the blown transformer and breakers and judged the power to be off. He was correct, wasn't he?"

Portman sucked in his lower lip before answering. "He would have been lucky. The transformer was for low voltage service to a house across the highway. It's unusual for it to blow all the breakers."

"Nevertheless, he judged correctly," Kellerman said.

"Yes, Sir. He did this time."

"Thank you," Kellerman said. He started to walk back to his table, then spun around. "Mr. Portman, you said if you were in a car with power lines on it, the best thing to do is stay put. Would that advice apply if the car was on fire?"

"No, Sir."

"If your family was in the car, would you chance the power lines to get them out?"

"Yes, Sir," Portman said quietly.

"Thank you." Kellerman returned to their table.

Alicia saw Buck's lawyer was frowning. Why did she have to choose a cunning lawyer like Bob Kellerman?

Clarence Brown stood again. "I'd like to call Rick Dupre to the stand."

Rick Dupre entered the courtroom. Tall and lean, he looked

handsome in his dress uniform. Alicia had come to know him through her friendship with his wife, Betty. Countless times, Rick had told her that Buck had done nothing wrong, but she'd refused to listen. Now she'd hear Rick tell the court, and she hoped the court believed him.

"What is your occupation, Mr. Dupre?" Clarence Brown asked.

"I'm a rancher and chief of the Muskrat Creek Volunteer Fire Department."

"How long have you been involved in fire fighting?"

Dupre rubbed his chin. "Pretty much all my life. I joined the Winnipeg Fire Department when I was twenty. I worked there for eleven years, then moved to Prince George where I served for another twenty years. Then I left fire fighting and went into ranching. I've been in charge of the volunteer department for another twelve years."

"Have you ever had experience with downed power lines at traffic accidents?" Brown said.

Dupre leaned forward. "More times than I can count."

"What is standard procedure?"

"Do nothing until the power company confirms that the line is no longer charged."

"Do you think this is a reasonable policy?" Clarence Brown asked.

"Absolutely."

"Why?"

"From personal experience," Dupre answered.

"Please tell us of that experience."

Kellerman stood so quickly that Alicia felt a small breeze. "Objection! Personal experiences are not evidence."

Judge Singh looked down from the bench and grinned. "I gave you plenty of latitude when it was your turn. Now it's Mr. Brown's turn. Please answer," he said to Rick Dupre.

"There was a car accident on the highway just outside of Winnipeg. The truck I was on was near the area and got there first. A high-voltage line was draped over the school bus and touched the ground. Kids were injured and screaming. We could see diesel fuel dripping out of the tanks. The car that hit the bus was in flames nearby. One of our guys ran to the bus and suddenly collapsed. Thinking he'd tripped, two more fire-fighters ran to help him. They collapsed too." Dupre stopped and rubbed his eyes.

"Why did they drop?" Clarence asked.

Dupre sucked in a breath, pain on his rugged face. "The line was live. The ground around the bus was energized. Two of those men died. The third was never the same." Dupre looked straight at Alicia. "That's why Buck did the right thing."

"What happened to the children in the bus?" Brown asked.

"Another fire truck came. We got a couple of hoses on the burning car, and the bus never caught fire. Those men didn't need to die."

"Thank you," Clarence Brown said.

Bob Kellerman stood and shuffled his papers. "Mr. Dupre, that is a deeply moving story, and I can understand why you feel the way you do. But isn't it a fact that firefighters take chances all the time? That the very nature of your job is risk taking?"

"Yes," Dupre said. "Calculated risks."

"And firefighters die after taking calculated risks, don't they?"

"Yes."

"And isn't it true," Kellerman said, "that firefighters have been known to approach downed power lines and effect res-cues that have saved many lives?"

"Yes," Dupre said.

"How did Buck Connelly get away with preventing Jeff

Thompson from taking a calculated risk which would have saved Garret Simmons's life?"

"Buck did the right thing," Dupre said.

"I'm sure in your mind he did. If Garret Simmons were here, he would probably feel differently."

Alicia watched as Clarence Brown called witness after witness, testifying to Buck's spotless character. None of them believed he was capable of such a heinous act as letting a man die. Finally, Clarence and Buck had a whispered conversation.

"Mr. Brown," Judge Singh said, "do you have any more witnesses?"

Brown slowly stood. "Yes, Your Honor. I call Buck Connelly to the stand."

Kellerman sat up straighter, satisfaction and anticipation oozing from him.

Buck walked forward, and the court clerk swore him in.

Clarence came near to the witness stand. "Buck, tell this court why you didn't let Jeff Thompson rescue Garret Simmons."

Buck looked at the judge. "A few months before the Simmons accident, I attended a car accident in another community. There were power lines draped over a car with injured people inside." A glistening sheen formed on his forehead. "The lines looked dead, so I grabbed my first aid kit and ran to the car. Just before I reached it, one of the lines arched and. . . ," Buck swallowed, "it got me; it burned me."

Clarence Brown leaned an arm against the oak railing around the witness stand. "So the fact that Garret Simmons was in the car had nothing to do with why you prevented Jeff Thompson from going down?"

Buck looked straight at Alicia. His eyes were sad, pleading. "No, it did not. The only reason I stopped Jeff was because he is my best friend. I couldn't stand to see him die. That's the truth."

"Thank you." Clarence Brown returned to his table.

Kellerman pressed close to Buck until he almost touched his shoulder. "Let me get this right. A live power line hit you, and now you're afraid of all power lines?"

Buck nodded. "Yes."

Kellerman smirked. "Isn't it true, that not too long after the Simmons accident, you attended a fire where horses were trapped in a burning barn, and you went in and rescued them?"

"Yes, though I didn't know there was fire until I got inside."

"Would that have mattered?"

"No."

Kellerman rubbed his forehead. "Let me get this right. You are afraid of power lines, but you'll risk your life for a bunch of dumb animals. Doesn't fire kill?"

"Yes, it does, but I understand fire. I can see it move. I know when it's going to strike. I can't do that with electricity."

A sarcastic smile crossed Bob Kellerman's face. "Would Garret Simmons's chances have improved had he been a horse?"

"That's enough," Judge Singh said. "Ask questions with answers I want to hear."

"Sorry, Your Honor." Kellerman pointed to Alicia and asked Buck, "Are you still in love with Alicia Simmons?"

Buck looked down.

"Mr. Connelly?" Kellerman said. "Please answer the question."

"Yes," Buck murmured.

"If she had been in that car instead of her husband, would you have stopped Jeff Thompson?"

Alicia locked eyes with Buck. She shook her head. *Don't say it,* her eyes pleaded.

"Yes," Buck said. "I would have stopped Jeff."

Kellerman walked toward Alicia. He rubbed his chin, then smiled. He turned to Buck. "You would have stopped Jeff. But would you have stopped yourself? Would you have stood there to watch Alicia Simmons die?"

Buck turned crimson. "I don't know," he gasped.

"Aw, come on," Kellerman said. "This is the woman you've pined for all your life. You'd watch her die? I hardly believe that. I'm finished, Your Honor." Kellerman returned to his seat, a smug expression on his face.

"Any more witnesses?" the judge asked Clarence Brown.

Clarence Brown stood, a slight smile on his face. "Just one more character witness."

Kellerman slapped his hand against the table. "Your Honor, we've heard plenty from character witnesses. Do we have to listen to one more?"

Judge Singh looked down from the bench. "I'm inclined to agree with you. Where are you going, Mr. Brown?"

"This witness is an expert, your Honor," Clarence said. "He's Buck Connelly's psychiatrist."

Kellerman jumped to his feet. "Objection! No psychiatrist was listed in discovery."

"Didn't know about him until yesterday," Brown said. "My client didn't tell me until then."

"And why did he keep this from you?" Judge Singh asked.

"May I approach the bench?" Clarence asked.

Kellerman followed Buck's lawyer. Angered whispers were all Alicia could hear. Kellerman did not look happy when he turned around. Alicia smiled.

Judge Singh pursed his lips. "I am going to allow this witness's testimony."

Kellerman muttered a curse and sat down.

"I call Dr. David Hickman to the stand," Clarence Brown said.

David Hickman looked nothing like a psychiatrist. He was broad shouldered, strong featured, and had an athletic build. He wore a sharp, dark suit, and his dark hair was cut short. His blue eyes were friendly as Clarence Brown approached him.

"Dr. Hickman, is Buck Connelly your patient?" Clarence Brown asked.

"Yes."

"And does he suffer from any mental health problems?" Brown asked.

"Yes."

"Would you explain his condition?" Clarence Brown returned to his table.

"Well, I should probably start with how we met," the doctor said. "I was called to an emergency at 100 Mile Hospital where I first met Mr. Connelly. He was curled up in a ball against the wall. He suffered from electrical burns, but the real damage was in his mind. It took three days of treatment just to get him to talk."

"You said he suffered from electrical burns. Could you elaborate on that?"

"Certainly. The power line hit him and knocked him to the ground. The line kept him trapped on the ground and struck him several times on the back before a RCMP officer had the good sense to use his shotgun to blow the transformer apart. Mr. Connelly was tortured for fifteen minutes before rescue."

Alicia looked over at Buck, her heart torn. It made sense now. Not once had he ever stripped off his shirt in front of her. What scars his back must hold.

"And what is the cumulative effect of this?" Clarence Brown asked.

"He has nightmares and a deep-seated fear of power lines."

"And that means what?" Clarence Brown asked.

"It means that Buck Connelly would have been incapable

of approaching power lines. The fear is too deep rooted. We've been working together on the problem, but Mr. Connelly has a long way to go."

Clarence Brown stood and approached Dr. Hickman. "You mean to say there's absolutely no way Buck Connelly could have gone near downed power lines."

"Pretty much," Dr. Hickman said.

"What about him stopping his friend from going down?" Clarence Brown asked.

"That would make sense. Buck Connelly sees power lines as a living threat. Since Jeff Thompson is his friend, he would try to stop his friend from approaching downed lines just like he would try and stop him from stepping in front of a train."

"Thank you. No further questions."

The judge turned to Kellerman. "Your witness."

Kellerman stood while Clarence Brown sat down. "You said, 'pretty much,' not yes, when asked if there was no way he could've approached those lines. That's not an absolute answer. Is there a case where he could overcome his fear? Like saving an injured man?"

Hickman shook his head. "No. It's a pervasive phobia. I mean, if it were his child trapped in a car, he might be able to overcome it, but not for a stranger."

Kellerman frowned. "Well, what about his ability to confront fire? Doesn't that seem strange?"

"No," Hickman said. "If a person is mauled by a dog, it doesn't mean he'll be scared of a horse."

Kellerman stiffened, as if he'd been slapped.

Kellerman cocked his head sideways. "Wait a minute. If Mr. Connelly is as terrified of power lines as you say, why was he still acting as a firefighter? Surely you must have discussed that."

"We did," the doctor said. "I suggested that he leave the department."

"And what did he say?"

"He said the Muskrat Creek department was undermanned and felt they would be better to have him the way he was than not at all."

Kellerman lifted his eyebrows. "And you agreed?"

"I did not," Hickman said. "It was my intention to have Mr. Connelly removed from duty."

"And why didn't you?"

"Because Mr. Connelly brought to me the *Manual of Fire Fighting Conduct*. In it, the procedure clearly states firefighters are not to approach power lines. Mr. Connelly's position was, since he's only afraid of power lines and firefighters aren't suppose to approach power lines, then there's no problem. I had to agree."

Kellerman looked like he'd been punched. He shook his head in disgust. "No further questions." He dropped back into his chair.

"Are you gentlemen prepared to give closing arguments?" Judge Singh asked.

"Yes, Your Honor," both lawyers replied.

Each lawyer briefly reviewed the testimony and showed how it proved his case. Kellerman pointed out Buck's obsession with Alicia, his bravery in other incidents, and the suspicious circumstances surrounding Garret's death. Clarence Brown emphasized that Buck followed correct procedure and, in any case, was incapable of performing the rescue.

"I'll render my decision a week from today." the judge tapped the gavel. "Adjourned."

ॐ

Half an hour later, Buck slipped into a restaurant booth across from Clarence and Paula. They'd already ordered him a cup of coffee. "How does it look?"

Clarence smiled. "He's toast. Dr. Hickman scuttled his case."

"What happens if I lose?"

"Not going to happen," Clarence said, "but if it does, the judge will determine monetary damages. I doubt they'll get two million, but a million isn't out of the question."

"Might as well be two million," Buck said. "I figure with the farm, livestock, and a few investments, I might be worth four hundred thousand, maybe five."

"If I know Bob Kellerman," Clarence said, "he's already done a search and probably has a better idea than you what you're worth. He'd clean you out."

Buck quirked his mouth. "Nice guy." He glanced at the door and saw Jeff walk in. His face was covered with sweat and soot. He beelined right for their table.

"I thought you were going to be at the trial today," Buck said. "From the looks of you, I'd say you were fighting a fire."

Jeff Thompson slid in beside him and grabbed a napkin to wipe his face. Streaks of soot quickly blackened it. "I was. Nasty one too."

"How bad was the damage?" Buck asked.

"House and barn. Fortunately, no one was hurt. And Buck?" He looked at his friend.

"Yeah?"

"It's on that same timber zone as the other two."

"No kidding," Buck said.

"What are you guys talking about, timber zone?" Paula asked.

"We had two—well, now three, fires," Buck said, "on the same side of the highway, all of the properties are close to each other. The first two have already sold to numbered companies," Buck said.

"Let me guess," said Clarence Brown, "for less than they were worth."

"No," Buck said, shaking his head, "for more than fair market value."

"Well, that's weird," Paula said. "Any idea who owns the numbered companies?"

Buck shrugged. "Not a clue. We searched the corporate records, and they led to a trust in the Cayman Islands. I hardly think Cayman bank officials will give out classified information to a farmer from Canada."

Paula rubbed her chin. "Hmm. They may not tell a farmer, but they might tell me."

Buck raised his eyebrows. "Are you serious?"

Paula smiled coyly. "In my years with the RCMP, I made a few overseas connections. Give me the numbers of the companies, and I'll let you know what I find out. Let's keep our eye on the third place that burned and see if it's snapped up."

"I'm going to do a little digging too," Clarence said. "Someone must know something about that area that isn't public knowledge. I've got a few political friends. I'll get them asking around."

"You know, Buck," Jeff said, "your place isn't far from the one that burned today."

Suddenly on high alert, Buck turned and faced his friend. "You think my place might be next?"

"Could be."

"I'll keep an eye out." Buck looked down at the table and frowned. "By this time next week, it probably won't be my place anyway."

sixteen

The next week dragged by. Neither Buck nor Isaac could do more than a minimum of work on the ranch. In spite of Clarence Brown's confidence, Buck was expecting the worst. The pending verdict hung over the ranch like a dark cloud though it had been sunny all week. A man took great pleasure in working on something that belonged to him, but Buck no longer had that assurance. In seven days, one man would decide if he was to lose everything he had worked so hard for.

On Wednesday, an appraiser hired by Bob Kellerman came to do a valuation of the ranch. When the stranger told why he'd come, Buck felt like tossing the thick-necked old timer out on his ear, but Isaac held him back. Isaac told Buck to trust the Lord and not the strength of his own arm. Buck reluctantly agreed and let the man look over the place. Later, Clarence Brown told him that Kellerman was entirely out of line.

Finally, Monday morning arrived. Judge Singh entered the courtroom at a minute before nine. He looked first at Buck, then at Alicia. "This has been a difficult case," the judge began. "I wrestled with this decision all week. To be honest, if this were a jury trial, I would suspect the jury would be deadlocked. Since it's not, I had to make a decision." He took a sip of water.

"First," he went on, "I would like to comment on the criminal aspect of this case. I can say clearly that had the RCMP proceeded criminally, they would have failed. There is definitely a reasonable doubt in my mind. There's sufficient evidence that Mr. Connelly may have been acting out of a desire to follow proper fire-fighting procedure."

Buck drew in the first full breath he'd taken since he woke up that morning.

"However," the judge said, "There is also evidence to indicate that Mr. Connelly acted out of self-interest when he kept Jeff Thompson from going down that embankment."

Buck held his breath in again.

"I found Dr. Hickman's testimony compelling. I did research during the week on conditions similar to Mr. Connelly's. I am convinced that Mr. Connelly's actions were not borne out of some desire to obtain Alicia Simmons, but the result of a horrific accident and injuries he received while trying to save lives at a previous event. My opinion is, Mr. Connelly is a brave man who needs time to heal. I am dismissing the claim."

Buck turned to Clarence and held out his hand, but his lawyer wrapped his arms around him. "Thanks, Pal," he said to the lawyer.

"Not a problem," he said.

Buck shook Paula's hand. "Thanks for your help."

"Glad to," she said. She looked past him. Buck turned around. Alicia stood, her arms loosely at her side. Kellerman was long gone. She took a step toward him.

"I'm sorry," she said. "I would've stopped this if I could have."

Buck wanted to wrap her in his arms, but that could never happen. "I know that." She held out her hand, and he gently shook it. Tears of joy were soon going to turn to tears of sadness. Alicia let go of his hand and walked out of the courtroom. Buck's gaze followed her all the way. *Lord, I don't suppose. . . ?*

ॐ

Buck screamed, and the snake bit into him again. He rolled onto his back, putting his arms up to fight it off. It kept coming and coming. He could fight no more.

He bolted up in bed, drenched in sweat. The dreams were less frequent, but they still came. The room was dark, with a dim moon glow coming through the window. The lighted numbers on his alarm clock told him it was four o'clock. There was no sense going back to sleep. The snake would just be there. He decided to get started on the animals. Since the trial began, Isaac had taken care of most of the chores alone. It was time Buck started doing his share.

After slipping on his jeans and flannel shirt, he moved quietly through the house. Buck pulled on his sheepskin jacket and shoved his stockinged feet into his boots. He opened the door and stepped out into the cool predawn air.

In the yard, Buck pulled in a slow, sweet breath. The aroma of hay and healthy animals filled his senses. Heading toward the barn, he decided to clean the horse stalls first. Maybe some time with his horses would help wash away the lagging nightmare.

A flickering light in the shop brought him out of his daydream. What in the world was Isaac doing up at this time? He froze, peering through the darkness. Jeff had warned him that this house might be next on the arsonist's list. Moving fast, Buck strode to the door of the shop. It was open a crack. He peeked in and saw the cutting torch burning next to the propane tank.

Flinging the door back, he rushed in and kicked the torch away from the tank. He quickly shut off the gas. It was completely dark in the shop now. He heard running footsteps behind him. Buck spun around in time to make out a dark shape framed in the doorway for an instant.

Buck charged out of the shop. In the dim moonlight, he spotted a figure heading toward the road. Whoever that man was, he was the key to everything. The toes of Buck's boots dug into the earth as he sprinted after the intruder. In ten strides, he closed the gap between them. Within two feet of the fleeing arsonist, Buck dove and dropped him with a tackle.

The man kicked out and caught Buck under the chin. Buck was stunned long enough for the man to get back up. Buck struggled to his feet, shadows of night spinning around him. Heavy shoes pounded across the yard. Blinking, Buck tried to locate the fleeing vandal.

"Get down!" Isaac's voice came from the porch.

Instantly, Buck flattened himself to the ground. *Boom!* The intruder howled. A second *boom*, and he dropped with a distinct thud.

Isaac stepped off the porch and came close to Buck. He spoke as though continuing a conversation with his boss. "Rock salt. Let's go see what we caught."

They carefully approached the groaning stranger.

"I heard you get up," Isaac told Buck as they walked. "I was just coming out to join you when I saw you chasing this guy. Lucky for him, I grabbed the gun with salt in it."

The man tried to stand, but Buck pushed him down with his foot. Buck clenched his fists and waved them over the man's face. "Stay where you are," Buck told him. "You'll be safer that way. If you get up, I'll knock you down again." He turned to Isaac and said, "Call the cops."

❧

The next morning, Alicia headed toward town. Sally was with Betty Dupre, who was taking a bunch of the kids into town to the swimming pool. Money was long gone now, and Alicia had heard of a new restaurant opening. Maybe with tips, it would be enough to keep the house.

Kellerman hadn't phoned, which was just fine with her. He was one man she never wanted to see again.

Shortly after she passed the fire hall, flashing red and blue lights appeared in her rearview mirror. She glanced at the speedometer, wondered what she'd done, and pulled to the side of the road.

A familiar-looking shape emerged from the police car. Alicia rolled down her window to see the grave face of Sergeant Meyers.

"I thought that was you," he said.

"Is something wrong?"

The sergeant nodded. "Could you come with me, please?"

❧

Over hot coffee at the kitchen table, Buck and Isaac were laughing and rehashing their adventure that morning. "I'll bet he feels like he's been sitting on a glowing woodstove," Isaac said.

"I know how he feels."

"Felt rock salt yourself a few times?"

Buck grinned. "Some friends and I were stealing eggs from the Markham farm. We wanted to throw them on Halloween. Old Mr. Markham came charging out of the house with his shotgun. I thought he was going to kill us until he lit up our rear ends with salt."

"Cured you of stealing eggs, didn't it?" Isaac asked, chuckling.

"That was the last time I even looked at another rancher's henhouse."

Isaac nodded. "Rock salt cured me too."

Buck lifted an eyebrow. "You've been shot with salt?"

Isaac grinned. "Every old man was once a boy."

A knock rattled the back door. "Wonder who that is?" Buck got up and opened the door. His face broke into a smile. "Paula, what brings you out here?"

Paula was grinning and tapping her foot. "Have I got something for you to see."

Buck stepped aside. "Come on in."

Buck led Paula into the kitchen. "Want a cup of coffee?" he asked.

"Sure." Paula set her leather bag on the table.

Another knock sounded at the door. "Busy place today," Buck said.

"I'll get the coffee." Isaac reached for the glass carafe.

Buck returned to the door and opened it to see Sergeant Meyers with Alicia. A frown crossed his face. What in the world could Meyers want? "Yeah?"

Pain flitted across Alicia's eyes.

"We need to talk," Sergeant Meyers said.

"Should I call my lawyer?" Buck asked.

Meyers replied, "This isn't about you, Mr. Connelly."

Buck looked at Alicia, fear charging through his veins. If it wasn't about him, who was it about? Was Alicia in trouble? *God, please, no.*

"Can we come in?" the sergeant asked again.

"Sure." Buck stepped aside. They entered, took off their shoes, and Buck led them into the kitchen.

"Quite a gathering we're having," Isaac said. "I'll put on more coffee."

"What's this about?" Buck asked, impatient to hear what was on Meyers's mind.

Sergeant Meyers thrust his hands into his pockets. "I've come to apologize. I brought Mrs. Simmons with me because I want her to hear this too. The man you caught last night is a known arsonist."

"Well, duh," Buck said. "He was trying to burn my place down."

"He's also a murderer," Meyers said. "We got a warrant and searched his apartment. We found a tube of glue that appears to be the same type used to tamper with the brake line of Garret Simmons's car."

Alicia's expression went blank. She swayed. Buck stepped across, caught her around the shoulders, and guided her to a chair. Having her that close did things to him. He had a hard time turning loose of her.

"That man murdered Garret," Alicia said.

Paula pulled a chair close to Alicia and put her arms around her.

"That's what we believe," Meyers said. "He's not talking now, but he will eventually. This proves conclusively Buck had nothing to do with your husband's death, Mrs. Simmons."

"I know that," Alicia said, her voice shaking.

"You do?" Buck asked, shocked.

She looked up at him and smiled weakly. "I was at the trial too, you know. When I saw you on the stand, I knew you were telling the truth. I believed you long before Dr. Hickman took the stand."

"Well, this all makes sense now," Paula said.

"What do you mean?" Meyers said.

"The murderer wasn't acting alone," Paula said. "It turns out Kellerman had more than just a huge fee as a reason to sue Buck."

"Are you saying Kellerman is involved?" Sergeant Meyers asked.

"I know it," Paula said. "My friends in the Cayman Islands traced down the owner of those numbered companies. It's a convoluted trail, but the man who owns them is a former business partner of Bob Kellerman's."

Sergeant Meyers let go a low whistle. "So he and Kellerman were working on this together."

"But why?" Buck wondered. "He paid fair market value."

Paula grinned. "Did he? This morning, Clarence heard from a friend in Victoria. The government is going to let the farms expand and remove the timber."

"Big deal," Buck said. "We still have to pay stumpage fees on the timber when we cut it. There wouldn't be enough money in it to risk arson."

"But there would be," Paula said. "Clarence pulled the original grants for the burned out properties and yours. These properties were part of a veterans' settlement project after the First World War. Each owner was granted not only the timber rights to his own land, but to the surrounding lands up to double the original parcel size."

"Why didn't anyone know about this?" Buck asked.

"Because hardly anyone ever reads old deed documents," Paula said. "Bob Kellerman did. It's in small print, but it's there. Once granted the agricultural lease rights, you could've removed the timber for free. These properties are worth millions."

Tears flowed freely down Alicia's cheeks. "Why did they kill Garret?"

"Your husband was on the council," Paula said. "He was also involved in real estate. When the first formal request came in, asking to log timber in this area, Garret must have stumbled across it. Once these guys start talking, I bet we'll find out that Garret was going to make the policy change public. They couldn't let him do that."

"My husband died for the sake of some trees?"

"There's a lot of money in timber," Paula said.

Sergeant Meyers moved toward the door. "I think I'll pay Bob Kellerman a visit." He looked at Alicia. "I'll drive you back to your car."

"I'll take her," Buck said. To his surprise, Alicia nodded.

"I've got to run. Mr. Kellerman might be hard to find, once this gets out." The sergeant banged the door shut behind him.

Alicia stood and walked over to Buck. "I'm so sorry," she said, lifting her face to him. "For what it's worth, I tried to stop him. I. . ."

Buck put his finger to her lips. "Let's go. We'll talk about it in the truck, okay?"

seventeen

As soon as Buck's truck touched the main road, Alicia said, "I told Bob Kellerman I wanted to drop the case. He threatened to sue me for his legal fees. He threatened to take my home. He even threatened to hurt Sally."

Buck's knuckles whitened on the steering wheel. "He threatened Sally?"

Alicia nodded.

"I'll rip his—"

"No, Buck," Alicia said, "don't even say it. There's been enough anger, enough hurt."

Buck took a couple of deep breaths and got his anger under control. "We should go get your car."

Here, sitting next to him, was the woman he loved. He would drive her to her car, she would get in, and that would be it. He wanted to do something, to say something, to see if there was any hope there. He glanced over at Alicia. She focused straight ahead. If only he could know what was in her mind.

They traveled down the highway and saw flashing lights in the distance.

"What's going on?" Alicia leaned forward to look around the cars ahead.

"It must be an accident." Buck felt at his belt for his pager, but of course, it wasn't there. The insurance company had made sure he'd never be a firefighter again. He stopped the truck at the end of a long line of vehicles. "I'm going to find out how long this is going to be." Buck reached for the door handle.

"I'd like to come," Alicia said.

He looked at her.

"Umm, I don't want to be alone."

Was that some sort of sign, Lord? She doesn't want to be alone, or she wants to be with me? They got out of the car and walked down the side of the highway. Rounding a short curve, they saw a crumpled minivan sitting thirty yards off the highway. "It must've rolled," Buck said, stopping.

Alicia reached for his hand and gripped it hard enough to hurt.

"What's the matter?"

"That's Betty Dupre's van. Sally's in there!"

Buck broke free from Alicia's grip and ran toward the group of firefighters. Like an old enemy, two power lines lay around the van, snapping and crackling, daring him to challenge them once more. Another truck lay nearby, burning. It was only a matter of time before those flames reached the minivan with Sally and the other children. He spotted Jeff and ran up beside him. "What are you guys doing?"

"Nothing," Jeff answered. "We're waiting for the power company."

"But the kids! The fire!" Buck shouted.

Jeff put his hands on Buck's shoulders. "Get a grip, Buck! The police have already locked Dupre in a patrol car because he tried to go rescue his wife. There's nothing we can do but hope the power company gets here before the fire gets to the van."

Alicia was at his side. "There's Sally!" She tried to run toward the van, but Buck grabbed her and hugged her close.

Buck could see Sally's face through the crackled glass. The roof of the van had been crushed, and there was no way anyone could get out. They'd have to be cut out. With the live power lines, no one could get close enough to do it.

The power lines coiled, then looked up and laughed at him. *Care to try again?* they taunted. *We got her husband, and now we're going to get her child. Maybe you too. Come on, Buck. Come play with us again.*

Buck looked at the power lines, then at Sally. Alicia writhed in his arms, crying a deep guttural moan. Her child was going to die in front of her. Sally was going to die. Little Sally, his friend—no, more than his friend. Buck had enough. Not this time.

Buck pointed to a rock outcropping about ten feet above the van. "It's okay, Alicia," he said. "I'll go get Sally."

"Not a chance," Jeff said. "Don't make me get the cops to lock you up too."

"Look at that," Buck said, still pointing. "I can jump from there onto the roof. The van is grounded, so I'll be safe. You can throw me down an air bottle and chisel, and I can cut a hole in the roof. You guys lower the rope. I'll harness up the kids and Mrs. Dupre."

"No way," Jeff said. "You could bounce off the van when you land on it. Not to mention, you might break your legs."

Buck looked at Sally's terror-stricken face. He'd rather be dead than watch her die. He shoved Alicia into Jeff's arms and sprinted to the rock outcropping. Voices called to him, but he ignored them.

Glad he didn't have any firefighter's gear on, Buck scrambled up the back of the outcropping. He glanced behind him to see the rest of the crew getting the gear he needed. A policewoman was holding Alicia, who was sobbing uncontrollably. Buck took a second to mentally distance himself from his torrid emotions. He had to stay calm and professional. Many lives depended on it.

On the edge of the rock, Buck looked down. Ten feet seemed a lot farther from up here. In order to hit the van and not roll off, he'd have to land with his feet, crouch, then fall to his hands. With a short prayer to carry him along, Buck jumped.

When his feet hit the van roof, the air gushed from his lungs. He slammed forward, and his wrists jolted hard, sending twin spears of pain up his arms. For a full minute, he lay there, trying to calm his pounding heart.

Slowly, carefully, he stood up. Above him, Jeff lowered the air tank and chisel. Buck grabbed them and fastened the hose of the chisel to the air tank. He opened the valve and started to work.

The air chisel functioned like a tiny jackhammer. The blade hammered into the thin metal of the van until he had cut open a hole big enough for him to fit through. He peeled the metal back, then cut through the support beams. With his knife, Buck sliced through the ceiling fabric and looked down at the crying children. He could see Mrs. Dupre in the front seat, blood dripping down the side of her head. She was moaning.

Sally yanked at her seat belt buckle, but it wouldn't release. He'd have to get the other kids out first. Buck grabbed a tow-headed ten-year-old boy, tied the lowered rope around him, and Jeff pulled him up. Next, Buck reached for a dark-haired girl, and she was soon in the arms of the firefighters up top. Buck climbed down into the van and cut Sally's seat belt loose.

"Buck," she sobbed. "I prayed, and you came."

She flung her arms around his neck. "I wasn't going to let you die like I did your father," he said, his lips pressed against her hair.

"You didn't let Daddy die."

"Who told you that?" he asked, fastening the rope around her.

"Mommy. She told me you were sick and couldn't save him."

"Well, I'm not sick anymore." He kissed Sally on the cheek and pushed her through the hole. While Jeff pulled her up, Buck glanced toward the fire trucks. Alicia was on her knees, waving at Sally and crying. Even if he died now, Buck's life was complete.

The smell of gas was becoming overpowering. The grass between the burning truck and the van caught fire. He only had seconds. He cut Betty Dupre's seat belt, pulled the lever, and the driver's seat fully reclined. Betty didn't weigh much more than a couple of hay bales. He worked the rope around her, scooped her from the seat, and pushed her through the hole.

He crawled out to the roof to wait for the rope to come back down for him. He heard a loud snap. An explosion of pain hit his side and propelled him off the roof, to the ground. As he rolled, he saw a jumping power line coming for him. Buck spun away as fast as he could, but the moving power line seemed to chase him. It got him this time. It was going to finish him off. At least he'd saved Sally. That was enough. The sparks came closer, and a blast deafened him. The exploding van had fragmented the live wire.

Water sailed over his head and engulfed the van. He heard a scream, and feet pounded the ground. The next moment, Alicia's face appeared over him. Her arms came around him. "Buck! I thought I'd lost you!" she cried, almost hysterical.

Buck was as close to heaven as he ever thought he'd get.

❧

Buck stood at the riding arena with his arm around Alicia's shoulders while they watched Sally ride Starfire. It was getting cold, but it wasn't cold enough to keep Sally off the pony. "That girl needs a father," Buck said.

Alicia folded her arm around his midsection and squeezed as she smiled up at him. "She's quite picky. Sally told me in no uncertain terms that she wants a father who can ride a horse, rope cattle, and save damsels in distress."

He gently pulled her around so she was facing him. "How

about her mother?" he murmured, his face close to hers. He loved to watch that sparkle in her hazel eyes.

For a moment, she hesitated. "I know I shouldn't ask this, but I have to know."

"What is it?" Buck asked, his eyes roving across her face.

"Why did you save Sally and not Garret? The psychiatrist said you were incapable of going near power lines."

Buck held Alicia's face in his hands. "Except for my own child."

A tear trickled down Alicia's cheek. "That's how you feel about Sally?"

"Yes," Buck nodded, "I love her as my own. And I love her mother every bit as much."

Alicia reached up and held his face in her hands and kissed him. "The girl needs a father."

"Is that a proposal?" he asked, grinning as he held her closer.

She leaned back to give him an arch look. "What do you think?"

Buck had promised God he wouldn't push Alicia, and God had answered back by wooing Alicia with the Holy Spirit. Now the way was clear for Buck to woo her himself. His answer: a sweet, slow, kiss.

A Letter To Our Readers

Dear Reader:

In order that we might better contribute to your reading enjoyment, we would appreciate your taking a few minutes to respond to the following questions. We welcome your comments and read each form and letter we receive. When completed, please return to the following:

Rebecca Germany, Fiction Editor
Heartsong Presents
PO Box 719
Uhrichsville, Ohio 44683

1. Did you enjoy reading *Flames of Deceit* by Rosey Dow & Andrew Snaden?

   ❑ Very much! I would like to see more books by this author!

   ❑ Moderately. I would have enjoyed it more if

   _____

   _____

2. Are you a member of **Heartsong Presents**? Yes ❑ No ❑
   If no, where did you purchase this book?_____

   _____

3. How would you rate, on a scale from 1 (poor) to 5 (superior), the cover design?_____

4. On a scale from 1 (poor) to 10 (superior), please rate the following elements.

   _____ Heroine   _____ Plot

   _____ Hero   _____ Inspirational theme

   _____ Setting   _____ Secondary characters

5. These characters were special because _____

_____

_____

6. How has this book inspired your life? _____

_____

_____

7. What settings would you like to see covered in future
   Heartsong Presents books? _____

_____

_____

8. What are some inspirational themes you would like to see
   treated in future books? _____

_____

_____

9. Would you be interested in reading other **Heartsong
   Presents** titles?   Yes ❏   No ❏

10. Please check your age range:
    ❏ Under 18   ❏ 18-24   ❏ 25-34
    ❏ 35-45   ❏ 46-55   ❏ Over 55

Name _____

Occupation _____

Address _____

City _____ State _____ Zip _____

Email _____

Seattle

Shepherd of Love Hospital stands as a
beacon of hope in Seattle, Washington. Its
Christian staff members work with each
other—and with God—to care for the
sick and injured. But sometimes they find
their own lives in need of a healing touch.

Can those who heal find healing for
their own souls? How will the Shepherd
for whom their hospital is named reveal
the love each longs for?

Titles by Colleen L. Reece

Lamp in Darkness
Flickering Flames
Kindled Spark
Hearth of Fire

paperback, 352 pages, 5 ³⁄₁₆" x 8"

❤ ❤ ❤ ❤ ❤ ❤ ❤ ❤ ❤ ❤ ❤ ❤ ❤

❤ ❤ ❤ ❤ ❤ ❤ ❤ ❤ ❤ ❤ ❤ ❤ ❤

Hearts♥ng

Any 12
Heartsong
Presents titles
for only
$30.00*

CONTEMPORARY ROMANCE IS CHEAPER BY THE DOZEN!
Buy any assortment of twelve
Heartsong Presents titles and
save 25% off of the already
discounted price of $3.25 each!

*plus $2.00 shipping and handling per order
and sales tax where applicable.

HEARTSONG PRESENTS *TITLES AVAILABLE NOW:*

(If ordering from this page, please remember to include it with the order form.)

·······Presents·······

Great Inspirational Romance at a Great Price!

Heartsong Presents books are inspirational romances in contemporary and historical settings, designed to give you an enjoyable, spirit-lifting reading experience. You can choose wonderfully written titles from some of today's best authors like Hannah Alexander, Andrea Boeshaar, Yvonne Lehman, Tracie Peterson, and many others.

When ordering quantities less than twelve, above titles are $3.25 each.
Not all titles may be available at time of order.